C

A Rainey Daye Coz

by

Kathleen Suzette

Books by Kathleen Suzette:

A Rainey Daye Cozy Mystery Series

A Pumpkin Hollow Mystery Series

Candy Coated Murder
A Pumpkin Hollow Mystery, book 1
Murderously Sweet
A Pumpkin Hollow Mystery, book 2
Chocolate Covered Murder
A Pumpkin Hollow Mystery, book 3
Death and Sweets
A Pumpkin Hollow Mystery, book 4
Sugared Demise
A Pumpkin Hollow Mystery, book 5
Confectionately Dead
A Pumpkin Hollow Mystery, book 6
Hard Candy and a Killer
A Pumpkin Hollow Mystery, book 7
Candy Kisses and a Killer
A Pumpkin Hollow Mystery, book 8
Terminal Taffy
A Pumpkin Hollow Mystery, book 9
Fudgy Fatality
A Pumpkin Hollow Mystery, book 10
Truffled Murder
A Pumpkin Hollow Mystery, book 11
Caramel Murder
A Pumpkin Hollow Mystery, book 12
Peppermint Fudge Killer
A Pumpkin Hollow Mystery, book 13
Chocolate Heart Killer
A Pumpkin Hollow Mystery, book 14

Strawberry Creams and Death
A Pumpkin Hollow Mystery, book 15
Pumpkin Spice Lies
A Pumpkin Hollow Mystery, book 16

A Freshly Baked Cozy Mystery Series

Apple Pie A La Murder,
A Freshly Baked Cozy Mystery, Book 1
Trick or Treat and Murder,
A Freshly Baked Cozy Mystery, Book 2
Thankfully Dead
A Freshly Baked Cozy Mystery, Book 3
Candy Cane Killer
A Freshly Baked Cozy Mystery, Book 4
Ice Cold Murder
A Freshly Baked Cozy Mystery, Book 5
Love is Murder
A Freshly Baked Cozy Mystery, Book 6
Strawberry Surprise Killer
A Freshly Baked Cozy Mystery, Book 7
Plum Dead
A Freshly Baked Cozy Mystery, book 8
Red, White, and Blue Murder
A Freshly Baked Cozy Mystery, book 9

A Gracie Williams Mystery Series
Pushing Up Daisies in Arizona,
A Gracie Williams Mystery, Book 1
Kicked the Bucket in Arizona,
A Gracie Williams Mystery, Book 2

A Home Economics Mystery Series
Appliqued to Death
A Home Economics Mystery, book 1

Table of Contents

Chapter One

"I WOULD KILL FOR ONE of those cupcakes," Arnold Singer said. He was stooped over, looking into the glass-covered display case, his eyes glued to the plate full of cupcakes I had just placed in it. He licked his lips, his eyes never leaving the cupcakes

I smiled, trying not to laugh. "They do look good, don't they?" I asked. "I got up early this morning to make them, but you don't have to kill for them. They'll only set you back a dollar."

He straightened up and narrowed his eyes at me. "Only a dollar?" he asked suspiciously. "That's all?"

I nodded. "I'm trying out cupcake recipes for my new cookbook. The only catch is that I need your opinion on them after you've tried one. I like constructive criticism, so don't hold back. If they're missing something, or they're too sweet, I need to know. I can't publish a cookbook with recipes that aren't as perfect as I can make them."

He licked his lips again, his eyes on the chocolate cherry cupcakes. Arnold was our mailman, and he still held the diner's

6

mail in his hand, apparently forgetting it was what he came in for.

He looked at me. "I'm not supposed to spend any money this week," he said sadly. "My wife keeps a tight hold on the checking account and she warned me three times this morning that this is a no-spend week." His eyes went to the cupcakes again, and he sighed.

Call me a soft touch, but I felt sorry for him. He really wanted a cupcake. "Well then, how about I just give you one?"

His eyes lit up. "Really? You can do that?"

I nodded, still trying to suppress a chuckle. Arnold was in his late forties, short, and what could best be described as portly. His close-cropped black hair was receding in front and his skin had a perpetually pink tone. "Sure, I can do that. I made them, after all. Which one do you want?"

He grinned, his thin lips stretching over his teeth. "I really couldn't ask you to do that. It wouldn't be right," he said, shaking his head.

"Arnold, I made these cupcakes primarily to get peoples' opinions on them. We're only charging a dollar because I need to buy more ingredients to make more of them as I continue to work on the recipe. Believe me, even at a dollar each, it will be more than enough money to buy more ingredients. Giving one away isn't going to leave me short. What I really want is input on them. I need that more than the money. Just promise to come back tomorrow and let me know how you liked it."

He grinned. "You're the best, Rainey! I have to deliver the mail anyway, so I can stop in tomorrow and tell you how it was. I'd like that one," he said, pointing to the fattest one in the bunch. The batter was cherry flavored, and it had chocolate frosting, cherry cream cheese filling, and a candied cherry sat on the top. I then topped it off with a drizzle of cherry syrup across the top.

"You got it," I said and handed him the cupcake. "You'll need some napkins." I held out three napkins to him.

He licked his lips and took the cupcake and napkins from me with his free hand. "You're the best, Rainey!" he said again. "This looks delicious."

I chuckled. "Thanks, Arnold. You can come and get a cupcake from me anytime. Just don't forget to stop back in and tell me what you think."

"You know I will. I'll see you tomorrow morning when I deliver the mail." He looked down at the mail he still held in his other hand. "Oh. I guess I better give you this."

"Thanks, Arnold," I said, taking the handful of mail from him. "I'll see you tomorrow."

"You got it, Rainey," he said and headed to the front door, whistling.

I looked through the mail he handed me and went back to the kitchen. My boss, Sam Stevens, was at the grill flipping pancakes.

"You're a soft touch, Rainey," he said over his shoulder.

"I know, I know. Arnold is a good guy, and he really wanted one of those cupcakes. I couldn't deprive him."

"Anything exciting in the mail?" he asked without turning around. Sam owned Sam's Diner and was a mellow boss to work for. His hair was growing too long again, and he wore it in a hair net these days.

"Only if you call the electric bill, a clothing catalog, and a grocery store flyer exciting," I said. "You might need to look elsewhere for excitement."

He snorted. "That electric bill will probably excite me, but in a bad way."

"I bet. I'll set it all on your desk," I said and headed to his office. Sparrow, Idaho hosted a busy tourist season during more temperate months with the Snake River drawing people to the excellent local fishing and camping. The diner was usually hopping during the tourist season, but winter had put a damper on things. We'd had a break in the weather the previous week, but it had turned cold again. I missed the blue skies of spring and summer.

"I see cupcakes!" Dianne Smith, the other waitress on duty said happily when I emerged from the office.

"You sure do. You better get one before they're all gone," I said. I was writing an Americana themed cookbook, and I frequently brought dishes for my co-workers to try out. Some of the food was sold and sometimes given, to customers. It gave me an opportunity to receive feedback on the food I made and was a big help in perfecting the recipes.

"Thanks, I need one. I skipped breakfast. If my kids saw me eat a cupcake this early, they'd point their fingers and tell me I'm not allowed to have sweets for breakfast, but I'm going to get one anyway," she said and headed back to the front counter. "Just don't tell them!"

"I promise not to tell," I said as I followed her back out front.

"Save one for me!" Ron White, our dishwasher called from his place near the sink.

"You got it!" I called back to him.

"What kind do we have here?" she asked, opening the display case.

"There's chocolate, cherry, and chocolate cherry," I said. "I think I'm going to make some lemon ones next. I've been craving lemon."

"I love lemon," she said, picking up a chocolate cherry cupcake. "Don't forget to bring them to work so I can try one."

"You know I won't," I said. Diane was one of my favorite people to work with. She was in her mid-forties and had been waitressing all her life. She was a professional and I could always count on her to more than pull her own weight when things got busy.

The bell above the door jingled and my boyfriend, Detective Cade Starkey, walked in. He smiled at me and headed over to the front counter and sat down. "What's up, buttercup?"

I giggled and leaned over the counter and kissed him. "Nothing."

"Hi Diane," he said, leaning to the side to see her standing behind me.

"Hi Cade. Look what I got," she said and held up the cupcake for him to see. She had taken a bite and the cherry filling was visible.

"Don't tease me. I want one of those," he said looking at me.

"Well, pick one out," I said, indicating the display case.

He stood up and looked at the cupcakes. "I want one like she's got."

I got him one of the cherry chocolate cupcakes and set it in front of him. "I'll get you some coffee," I said and headed to the coffee pot. I heard the bell jingle over the door and Diane greeted the customers that came into the diner.

"Wow," Cade said, his mouth full of the cupcake when I returned with his coffee.

I set the cup in front of him. "Is it any good?"

He made a circle with his finger and thumb, nodding, and took another bite. "The best," he said around the food in his mouth.

"Well you better order some protein to go with that, or you're going to end up with low blood sugar," I warned. "Sugar on its own this early isn't good for you."

"Yes, Ma'am," he teased and saluted me. "How about scrambled eggs and toast?"

I chuckled. "For some weird reason I knew you were going to say that. It's like I'm psychic or something," I said and pulled my order book from my apron pocket and jotted down his order. Cade was a man of few tastes in the morning. Scrambled eggs and toast were his usual fare.

"You're a genius," he said and took a sip of his coffee. "Boy, this cupcake is good."

"Thanks." I headed back to the kitchen with the order ticket. "Sam, Cade's here," I said.

"Scrambled eggs and white toast it is," he said without looking at the order.

I hung the ticket up anyway. "There are a couple more customers out there, so maybe things are going to pick up today."

"I hope so. I've been considering discontinuing the clam chowder for a while. Even with the smaller pots I've been making, we've had leftovers."

"Maybe you should completely scale down the menu during the winter," I suggested. "Just make the items that sell the most and advertise that that's what you're doing so people know they can still get their favorites, but not some of the other items."

"I had the same idea. March will be here soon and business usually picks up toward the end of the month. Maybe I'll plan to do that next year. That will give me plenty of time to let people know," he said, cracking eggs into a bowl.

"That's a great idea," I said and popped two slices of bread into the toaster.

"Hey Rainey, will you make chocolate turtle cupcakes next?" Ron asked as he rinsed a plate and set it in the drying rack.

"That sounds really good. I don't think I've ever made turtle cupcakes before," I said. "I'm going to have to look into that."

"See? I've got good ideas," he said without looking at me. "You could pay me in cupcakes for those ideas."

"I might just do that, Ron." When Cade's breakfast was ready, I took it out to him and set it down on the counter. "Here we are."

"Mm, Scrambled eggs and toast," he said, picking up his fork.

I glanced over at the display case. "Wait a minute, something's not right here," I said. There were four cupcakes missing from the cake stand. "Let's see, I gave Arnold a cupcake,

Diane took one, and you took one. And yet, there are four cupcakes missing from the display."

"I don't know what you're talking about," he said as he scooped eggs onto a piece of toast.

I narrowed my eyes at him. "I think you do."

The door swung open before I could accuse him of eating two cupcakes. "Hello folks," I said to the party of three that walked through the door.

Chapter Two

AS SOON AS I HAD SERVED Cade his breakfast, it seemed someone had put the word out that there were free cupcakes at Sam's. We suddenly had a steady stream of customers, most of them asking for those free cupcakes.

"I'm sorry, Stephanie, but we don't have any free cupcakes," I explained. She was the seventh customer that had asked. I refrained from looking over my shoulder at the covered cake stand that still held half a dozen cupcakes. I knew who was spreading the word of course, and I intended to have a word with him when he stopped in tomorrow to drop off the mail.

Stephanie Fabrezeo's face fell. "Really? Are you sure? Because my mailman, Arnold Singer, said there were free cupcakes at Sam's." She peered around me and looked at the covered cake stand. "Are you sure there aren't any free cupcakes?" she asked again.

"Well, there aren't any free cupcakes, but we do have some for a dollar apiece," I said. "Would you like to buy one?" I had convinced four of the previous six customers to buy one. I felt like the odds of getting someone to pay for them was relatively high, but I had caved to Mr. and Mrs. Morgan. They were elderly and had looked so disappointed at having come out in the cold for free cupcakes that didn't exist. I just couldn't tell them they had to pay, especially after they mentioned they lived on a fixed income. Three times.

Stephanie's face fell. "Oh. A dollar? I know that isn't much, but my memaw's birthday is today and she so wanted a birthday cake, but I told her she couldn't have it because her blood sugar has been high lately." Stephanie was forty-six and ran the local used clothing store. Proceeds benefited a local cat shelter. Her long curly red hair had faded in color and she was painfully thin, with her collar bones jutting out sharply beneath her skin.

I glanced at Cade, who was grinning at me and watching this thing unfold. "Oh, well, if her blood sugar is high, it's probably best not to eat cake." I wondered if she was under the mistaken impression that the cupcakes were sugar-free.

"That's right. I told her I'd get her a cupcake instead. At least that way, she'll only eat a little bit of sugar and not a great big piece of cake. There's too much sugar in cake." She looked at me and nodded as if this made sense.

I gave Cade a sideways glance. I couldn't help it. But that was my first mistake because he had his head down and his shoulders were shaking. Seeing him try to hold the laughter in made me want to laugh, and I bit my lower lip so I wouldn't embarrass myself.

I caved. "Well then, why don't you take her a cupcake? It's her birthday, after all," I finally said and got one of the cupcakes for her along with some napkins. I handed it to her, and she stood there in front of me without making a move.

She looked at me, cupcake in hand. "I need two. She can't eat a cupcake by herself. It wouldn't be right."

I smiled and considered telling her that since it wasn't *her* birthday, she would have to buy one for herself. Then I caved again. At this rate, I had less than a fifty percent success rate in selling cupcakes. Arnold was going to get a piece of my mind. I opened my mouth to say something, then thought better of it. "Of course," I said and got another one out for her. Stephanie was a little air-headed, and I hoped her memaw would survive the cupcake and not go into a sugar-induced coma.

"Thanks, Rainey. You're so nice," Stephanie said and headed for the door with the two cupcakes.

"You're welcome, Stephanie. I've got some things I want to drop by your shop later. You can tell me how you and your memaw enjoyed the cupcakes."

Cade bellowed with laughter when the door closed behind her. "That was great! You probably killed Memaw with your cupcakes."

"Hush up, Cade," I growled. "Darn that Arnold. Now I'm out the money for the next batch of cupcakes. I ought to throttle him when I see him next."

"Come on, Rainey. Just think of it as a compliment. People are braving the cold weather to get one of your cupcakes," he said.

I smiled and shook my head. "Yeah, but I don't have the time to track everyone down and ask them how they liked the cupcakes. I bet they wouldn't brave the cold if they had heard they weren't free."

"They were excellent. Take my word for it," he said and drained his coffee cup. "One more for the road?" He held up the cup.

"Sure," I said and took it from him.

"Hey Rainey," Luanne called from the kitchen. "Can I have a cupcake?"

"Sure, but you better get one quick. They're going like hotcakes." I refilled Cade's cup and brought it back to him.

"Yum, I love cherry cake," Luanne said, picking out a cherry cupcake. "I'm glad I came in early or I might not have gotten one. I came in early so I could go home early, by the way."

"I thought you had the lunch shift? It's not quite 9:00," I said and set Cade's cup down in front of him.

"Yeah, that's why I came in early. So I can go home early. I have an appointment at 12:30."

I eyed her as she took a bite of the cupcake. I was not going to stay and work the lunch shift for her. Georgia Johnson would be here then and she and I had issues. She couldn't stand me and I had no idea why, and I had an issue with that.

I turned to look at Cade when his phone went off. He sighed and pushed his plate away. I picked the plate up, but he made no effort to pull his phone from his pocket and answer it. He leisurely took a sip of his coffee.

"Don't you care who's calling you?" I asked him.

He shrugged. "I suppose I should, but I don't. I need to get back to the office, but I don't want to do that, either."

"Well, I'm off at 11:00, we can go to Agatha's and get a coffee. You can hang out until then, I guess," I said and took his plate back to the kitchen.

"Are we out of cupcakes?" Sam asked, wiping his hands on the white apron he wore tied around his waist.

"Almost. Here you go, Ron." I set the dirty plate on the sideboard.

"I had a cupcake, they were great," Ron said, reaching for a pot to wash, the faded hula girl tattoo on his arm moving with his flexing bicep. "Reminds me of my mother's cupcakes. My mother was a good cook and baker."

"Thanks, Ron. Makes me proud to hear that." I headed back out front. Cade still hadn't moved, but his phone had stopped ringing. "What do you say about that coffee later?"

"Sounds good," he said as his phone started ringing again. He sighed and reached into his coat pocket and removed the phone. When he looked at it, his brow furrowed. "It's your Mom."

"My Mom calls you?"

"Sure. Sometimes we discuss pottery." He answered the phone. "Hi Mary Ann," he said and then was silent a few seconds.

Smart aleck. I saw how I rated.

"I'll be right there. Don't do a thing," he said into the phone.

"What's going on?" I asked when he hit end.

"Your mom says there's a dead man parked on the side of her house," he said.

"What?" I said in disbelief. "What do you mean a dead man is parked on the side of her house?"

He shrugged and stood up. "That's what I'm going to go find out. Tell Sam I'll pay for breakfast later."

"I'm going with you," I said. "Let me tell Sam."

I ran back to the kitchen. "Sam, I have a family emergency. I've got to go."

He turned toward me, eyebrows raised. "Okay. Let me know if everyone's okay," he said.

"I will. And Cade will pay for his breakfast later." I didn't wait for an answer. I grabbed my purse from the backroom and ran to catch Cade. He'd leave without me if I didn't hurry. He didn't always appreciate my help when dead people showed up.

I climbed into the front seat of his car and slammed the door. "What did she say? What dead guy?"

"She said the mailman is dead, and he's parked near the side of her house," he said and started the car. The roads were thankfully clear, and he pulled away quickly.

"Wait. Not Arnold."

"She didn't say."

I had lived with my mother when I moved home from New York the previous year. Arnold was her mailman. I bit my lip, suddenly feeling queasy. I hadn't looked at the clock when he was at the diner, but it couldn't have been much more than an hour since he had stopped in.

"Did she say what happened to him?"

"No, only that she went out to her car, and saw the mail truck idling against that cinder block wall that separates the houses on her block from the highway. When she went to see if he was okay, she realized he was dead."

I sighed. Poor Arnold.

Chapter Three

MOM WAS STANDING ON her porch when we got to her house, her arms wrapped around herself. Cade pulled into Mom's driveway and parked.

"Where is he?" Cade asked when we got out of the car.

"He's around the side there," Mom said, walking down her porch steps and motioning to the side of her house. Mom lived on the edge of town and there was a dead-end road that ran along the side of her house that was rarely used. It stopped at a cinderblock wall that ran behind the houses, separating them from the highway. "I tried to wake him up, but he didn't move. He has some kind of dark substance on his face. Maybe he was bleeding internally, and he vomited?"

Cade nodded and headed around the side of the house. The mail truck wasn't far from the house and I could hear the low hum of its still running motor. The driver-side window was rolled down, and he reached in and felt Arnold's neck for a pulse. Mom came to stand beside me in the driveway, her face creased with concern. I folded my arms in front of myself and watched Cade.

"Did he crash into the wall?" I asked her.

"I never heard it hit. There isn't much damage to the front of the mail truck."

"Huh. Maybe he got sick or something," I said.

"Poor thing," Mom clucked. "Could be he had a burst aorta or a heart attack or something."

"I just spoke to him about an hour ago when he brought the mail into the diner," I said. "How sad."

She nodded. "He was always so nice. He brought the mail up onto the porch when there was a large package instead of leaving me a call ticket to pick it up at the post office. You wouldn't catch Gina Grand doing that. She's too lazy to get out of the mail truck."

I nodded. "He was a really nice guy." Cade made a phone call and looked in our direction. When he got off the phone, he headed over to us.

"What's that dark substance on his face?" Mom asked him.

"Looks like frosting," he said, looking at me.

I gasped. I knew what he was thinking. "I did not kill him with my cupcake."

He shrugged and smiled. "I've always said you make a killer cupcake, but I didn't mean it literally."

"You're so funny," I said and slapped his arm.

"Rainey, it seems like you could be more careful about what you put into your baked goods," Mom said, shaking her head. "Poor thing. All he wanted was something sweet, and this is how you repay him."

Cade snickered.

"Stop it!" I said in exasperation. "It isn't funny. Poor Arnold is dead and you two are making jokes."

He turned to me and became serious. "You're right. There's nothing funny about it. It looks like there's a bullet wound to his chest, but we'll have to wait on the medical examiner's report to know for sure."

"A bullet wound?" I said. "In this neighborhood?"

He nodded. "He didn't even finish his cupcake. There's a piece of it on the seat beside him."

"Oh," I said sadly. "He really wanted that cupcake. Mom, did you hear a gun go off?"

"No, I didn't hear a thing," she said, shaking her head. "I can't imagine who would be shooting up the neighborhood. I always thought that Betty Allen down the street was running a crack den. Maybe it was a drug deal gone wrong."

I narrowed my eyes at her. Betty Allen was a minister's wife. "Wait a minute. Why aren't you at work?" I asked.

She looked at me sheepishly. "I needed a break, so I came home for a few minutes."

That didn't make sense. My mother owned a florist shop, and she was nearly always there during business hours. "What kind of break? And for how long?" I asked. "The mail truck wasn't there when you got home?"

She shrugged. "Since when do I have to tell you my personal business?" she asked. "You sure are nosy."

Cade chuckled.

"Since I'm your daughter and I want to know why you'd be home at this hour of the morning when you should be working," I said, and leaned on Cade's car. Sirens were heard in the distance. They could have saved them. Poor Arnold was in no hurry.

She sighed. "I did not kill Arnold if that's what you're asking. Are you asking me that?"

"Don't jump to conclusions, Mom. I'm not asking anything of the sort. Why are you avoiding the question?"

Before she could answer, my identical twin sister, Stormy, drove up and parked next to Cade's car. She got out of her car and glanced in Arnold's direction. "What's going on?" she asked. "Was there some kind of group meeting that I wasn't invited to?" She gave us a cheesy grin and glanced at Arnold's mail truck again. "Did the mailman run into the wall?"

"Arnold Singer's dead," I told her.

Her head whipped around to look at me. "Seriously? Arnold the mailman? What happened?"

"Someone shot him dead. That or Rainey poisoned him with a cupcake and he shot himself. We aren't sure yet," Mom said.

"Mom! Stop it!" I hissed. I turned to Stormy. "Mom just found him out there."

"We are of course, going to investigate," Cade said and walked back over to the mail truck as the first police cruiser showed up.

"Did you hear anything?" Stormy asked our mother.

She shook her head. "Not a thing. I was coming out of the house to go back to work, and I heard a motor running. I went over and took a look. Arnold didn't seem to be moving, so I checked on him to be sure he was okay. He was already dead, with a mouthful of one of Rainey's cupcakes."

"How sad," Stormy said. "I wonder what happened?"

"All we know is that Cade said he has what looks like a gunshot wound to his chest," I said.

Stormy mirrored me and crossed her arms in front of herself. "Arnold was always so sweet in a geeky way. I just can't imagine someone wanting to kill him," she said.

"I know who would want to kill him," Mom said, nodding her head.

We both turned to look at her. "Who?" I asked.

"Everyone he delivered mail to. People get tired of having bad news delivered to their doorstep. Someone probably just had enough of it and shot him."

Stormy and I sighed loudly. "Really Mom? Because that's how you get the bills to stop coming—by shooting the messenger." What I said hit me, and I rolled my eyes at myself.

Two more police cruisers showed up, and the ambulance wasn't far behind. My mother's next-door neighbor peeked out from behind her curtains to watch what was going on. I felt bad for Arnold, especially since we had just had a conversation this morning. He came into the diner every day to drop the mail off, but depending on how busy we were, we didn't always speak other than to say hello.

"Mom, how did you not hear a gunshot?" Stormy asked, turning to her.

She shrugged. "I was in the kitchen using the blender. I didn't hear anything. I feel sorry for his wife, Adele. They live down the street and two blocks over, you know."

"I hadn't realized that," I said. "Does she still work at the county library?"

"Yes, she's been a librarian for years," Mom said. "At Christmas time she brought me a plate of fudge. It was delicious. Good neighbors are hard to find."

Cade walked back over to us. "Would any of you happen to know who Arnold's next of kin is?"

"Yes, his wife works at the county library," I said. "Mom said she lives a couple of blocks over. Adele Singer."

He nodded and wrote down the address that Mom gave him. "She's probably at work. I'll stop by the library."

"The poor thing," Mom said. "I'd hate to get that news."

Cade nodded. "It's not something anyone wants to hear. I'll call you later," he said to me.

With a quick kiss, Cade was gone. The emergency vehicles would be here for a while, so we all went inside to wait until they were finished looking the area over and removed Arnold's body.

"Who wants tea?" Mom asked.

"Tea sounds good," I said. "I feel terrible about what happened to Arnold."

"I can't imagine who would kill Arnold," Stormy agreed as we followed Mom into the kitchen.

Mom opened a cupboard door and pulled out two boxes of tea. "Orange spice or English breakfast?"

"Orange spice for me," I said.

"Orange spice sounds good," Stormy said as she went to the stove and turned on the burner beneath the teakettle.

"I'll tell you one thing," Mom said as she took out the tea infuser and filled it with orange spice tea. "It's a brave person that will shoot someone dead in the middle of the street in the middle of the day. This isn't a bad neighborhood."

"You can say that again," I agreed. Whoever had killed Arnold had no fear of being caught. While most people in the neighborhood worked, there were a handful of people that didn't. And besides that, even if people did work, there was no way for the killer to know whether everyone was gone or not.

"The thing is," Stormy said turning to me. "Arnold was a sitting duck. He runs the same route every day at approximately the same time. It wouldn't have been hard for the killer to find him."

"And Arnold was a stickler for his schedule. I can almost time it to when he would be dropping the mail off. It was usually between nine o'clock and nine-thirty. But usually closest to nine-fifteen," Mom said, nodding.

When the water boiled, Stormy poured it into Mom's porcelain teapot and Mom added the tea infuser and we headed to the table to sit down.

"What's going on over there?" Stormy asked as we waited for the tea to steep.

We all looked out the large kitchen window and over at Mom's neighbor's house. The dirt road Arnold's mail truck had rolled down was between Mom's and Alice Garber's house and now Alice was crouched down at the corner of her house, watching the police and EMTs as they waited for the coroner. Mom's house was a Victorian-style that she had been slowly restoring over the years. Her kitchen had large windows, and on one side we could see her neighbor's house and that dirt road.

"Oh, you know how Alice is," Mom said, chuckling. "She's always been an oddball. She probably thinks the neighborhood is being invaded with all those flashing lights and men in uniform."

Stormy chuckled. "The sad thing is, she probably does think that."

I watched Alice for a moment while Mom poured the tea. "She does behave oddly, doesn't she?"

"Just last week there were a couple of cats fighting in her backyard, and she called the police over it. She thought there were people in her backyard beating each other up."

"Really?" I asked thinking about this. "I guess her mind is deteriorating a bit?"

Mom nodded and poured tea into her cup. "Maybe, but sometimes I think she just does it for the attention."

"I'd hate for her to be calling the police out to her house if she was just doing it for attention," Stormy said. "I would think the police would put a stop to it if they thought that was the case."

"I warned her about doing that," Mom said. "But she doesn't listen to anyone."

Alice had two adult children, and I wondered if they checked up on her very often if she was resorting to calling the police just to get attention.

Chapter Four

AN HOUR AND A HALF later I saw Cade return and park out front. The coroner arrived after him and parked behind his car. I was surprised the coroner had shown up as early as he did. It sometimes took hours for him to arrive. I didn't know if that was because he had other dead people to check out, or he just didn't enjoy what he did for a living and was dragging his feet.

"I'd hate to have Cade's job," Stormy said as she took a sip of her now cold tea. "I can't imagine having to tell someone their loved one has died. Especially if they were murdered."

Alice Garber had given up her perch at the corner of her house a half an hour earlier and had gone back inside. I was pretty sure she was hovering somewhere near a window though.

When we finished with our tea, and Arnold's body was loaded into the coroner's van, we walked out onto Mom's front porch. Cade saw us and walked over to us. "I'm going to ask around at the neighbor's houses and see if anyone heard or saw anything."

"Most of my neighbors work, but we saw Alice Garber watching what you all were doing," Mom said, indicating the green house next door. "She's kind of eccentric and keeps to herself while keeping an eye on the neighborhood. It's a good bet that she may have seen something suspicious."

"I'll start with her, then," he said and headed toward her house.

I followed after him. "Alice doesn't let much get by her," I whispered. She also had ears that could hear a pin drop in the middle of the Super Bowl while the crowd was roaring.

He glanced at me. "Somehow I knew you'd tag along."

I snickered. "That's because you're so smart."

"I'm a regular genius when it comes to knowing what you might do."

He rang Alice's doorbell, and we waited. After a few moments, the door slowly opened. She looked from me to Cade and back, then smiled tentatively, but didn't appear to recognize me. "Hello."

"Hi Alice, I'm Mary Ann's daughter, Rainey. Do you remember me?"

"Of course I do," Alice said, narrowing her eyes at me. "I just couldn't figure out which one you were." Alice was only in her early sixties, but she sometimes acted older. I suspect it was because of her reclusive nature.

"My name is Detective Cade Starkey, Ma'am," Cade said and stuck his hand out to shake hers. "We'd like to ask you if you saw or heard anything unusual in the neighborhood this morning."

She made no effort to shake his hand. "No, I can't say that I did," she said and peered around Cade. "What happened to Arnold?"

"There was an accident," Cade said, pulling his hand back. "That's why we're asking if anyone saw anything."

She shook her head, her eyes still on Arnold's mail truck. "Arnold's dead, isn't he?"

"Yes, Ma'am, he is," Cade said somberly. "Are you sure you didn't hear or see anything suspicious this morning?"

She made a clucking sound. "Doesn't surprise me a bit. I knew one day he'd get himself into trouble."

Cade glanced at me. "What do you mean by that?"

She shook her head and grimaced. "Everyone knows a mail carrier's job is dangerous. I warned him about being careful, but did he list to me? No. He didn't ever listen to me."

"Was there something specific that you were worried about? Was there anyone that you thought might want to harm Arnold?" Cade asked her.

She shook her head. "Of course not! Who on earth would want to harm Arnold?"

Cade looked at me, surprised, and I shrugged. I knew Alice was eccentric, but I didn't think she was out of her mind. At least, I was pretty sure she wasn't, but I may have been wrong.

"Alice, can you explain why you thought Arnold might get into trouble?" I asked her.

She was holding the door close against her body so that she could just squeeze through as she spoke. "What are you talking about? I didn't say anything like that. Why would I think that?"

My mouth dropped open. "Alice, you just said you thought Arnold might get into trouble. And we were just wondering why you thought that."

"This is a quiet neighborhood. I don't know why anyone would go around murdering anyone else. But you know how the world is these days. It seems that no one values human life and somebody my age has seen a lot, I'll tell you. But, it's going to be up to lawmakers to make sure that the guilty party is held accountable for their actions," she said looking at Cade.

Cade looked as confused by her behavior as I was.

He sighed. "Yes ma'am," he said, agreeing with her. "We're doing everything we can to make sure this is a safe neighborhood. In light of what has happened here today, we would appreciate any and all information you or any of your neighbors could give us regarding Arnold Singer. Now, are you sure that you didn't hear or see anything earlier today?"

She inhaled deeply. "Detective, I neither saw nor heard anything. I hope it won't take you long to find that killer. We can't live with killers on the loose."

Cade nodded and sighed again. "Let me give you my business card, and if you remember anything, would you please give me a call?" He reached into his coat and pulled out a business card and handed it to her.

She looked at the card suspiciously before taking it from him. "I certainly will." Without another word she took a step back and slammed the door in our faces.

Cade and I turned to look at each other. "Well, Mom did say she's a bit eccentric, didn't she?"

"She did say that," he said, and we headed back over to my mother's house.

The police were pulling away as we got back to Mom's doorstep. "Did Alice have anything to say that might help you, Cade?" Mom asked.

He looked at her blankly. "I'm not really sure. It was a confusing conversation."

Mom laughed. "Cade, would you like some tea? I put a pot on earlier and I can warm it up for you," she offered.

Cade looked up at the darkening sky. "I really shouldn't," he said and looked back at Mom. "But maybe I'll take one cup."

We all went back into the house and into the kitchen. Mom poured a cup of tea for Cade and put it into the microwave to warm it up.

"Tea is best when it's freshly brewed," she said. "But it won't hurt it to be warmed up."

"I appreciate it," Cade said and took a seat at the table. Cade was quiet a few moments, deep in thought.

"I just can't imagine someone coming into this neighborhood and shooting somebody right out in the open like that," I finally said.

He nodded. "You never can tell with some people," he said. "It could've been a spur of the moment decision, or it may have been something well-planned. Could be they were just driving by and saw him out on his mail route and decided today was the day. The neighborhood was quiet and appeared to be empty, and they took advantage of that."

"Like Mom said earlier, they knew where to find him. He was a stickler for making his mail deliveries on time," I said. "I just don't know what's going on with Alice. She acted really odd."

"Some days she seems with it, and some days she doesn't," Mom said with a shrug. "But like I said before, I really think most of it is a ploy for attention."

"Well if it's a ploy for attention," I said. "Then it's kind of sad. A person shouldn't have to feel they've got to behave that way to get some attention. Where are her kids? Have they been around lately?"

Mom shrugged. "I haven't seen them, but they might come around while I'm at work."

I eyed my mother. "You never did say why you were home today." It wasn't like my mother to stay home during the day if she wasn't sick and she looked healthy to me.

She went to the microwave and got Cade's tea. "There wasn't much to do at the shop today. The girls can handle it."

I turned to Stormy. She arched one eyebrow and turned to Mom. "What's going on? Quit avoiding the question."

I smirked at my sister. She was usually the kind and gentle one, but she knew as well as I did that something was up with Mom.

Mom sighed and sat at the table. "Things have been a little slow at the shop is all. I've got Donna and Vicky to do what work there is, so why should I be there?"

I was surprised by this. "Valentine's Day is just over a week away. Isn't that the busiest time of the year for florists?" I asked.

"It is," she said and nodded but didn't say anything more about it.

"The new florist shop is really hurting your business, then," I said and looked at Stormy. The Happy Petals florist shop had opened last fall and Mom had been quiet about it. I hadn't worried too much since Mom had been in business for years and was well-liked in the community, but Happy Petals was her only competition. The Perfect Flower Shop had closed with its owner's demise early last year and Mom had had the flower market cornered until the new shop opened.

"I wouldn't say it's hurting my business," she said without looking at either of us. "You know how it is being in business for yourself. There are slow times and more prosperous times. It happens."

I bit my lip and didn't bring up the fact that this month should have been booming for her. But maybe when we got closer to Valentine's Day, she would see an uptick in sales.

"I'm sure things will turn around," Cade said and took a sip of his tea. "I've only heard good things about your flower shop since I came to Sparrow. People like you and the work you do, Mary Ann."

Mom smiled at the compliment. "Thanks, Cade. I knew I liked you."

Stormy's eyes met mine, and I saw the worry. I gave her a slight nod. It would kill Mom to admit she was struggling if that was what was happening, but we would pin her down and get details from her when Cade wasn't here. She had too much pride to admit it in front of him.

Chapter Five

MOM AND I DECIDED TO stop by to see Adele Singer the following morning. I had made some lemon cream cupcakes and brought some along for her.

"I hope you saved some of these cupcakes for me," Mom said from the passenger seat. She held the plate of cupcakes in her lap. "I can smell the lemon through the plastic wrap, and it smells delicious."

"I'll make another batch," I said. "I dropped the rest of them off at the diner on my way over to your house. I made a wonderful lemon cream that I put in the center of them. I think they might be my best cupcakes ever." They would make a great addition to my cookbook and I was pleased they had turned out so well on the first try.

When we pulled up to Adele's house, Mom, and I stared. It was then I realized that I hadn't driven by her house in years. Or maybe I had never driven by it because if I had, I would have remembered it. I had never seen so many garden gnomes in one place. We sat at the curb with the engine idling as we took it all in. There were gnomes all over the planters and the front yard, along with a dozen large wooden people-shaped cutouts. The crown jewel was the classic wooden grandma bent over with her bloomers showing for all the world to see.

"There has to be at least a hundred gnomes," Mom said slowly. "Who has that many gnomes?"

I shook my head slowly and remembered my car was still running. I put it in park and shut off the engine. "How have we missed this? She only lives two blocks away and around the corner. How did we not know this was here?"

Mom shook her head. "I have no idea. I guess I don't drive down this street often. Or maybe never. Why do you think there are so many gnomes?"

"I don't know. And why does she have so many of those big wooden people in her yard?" I asked. It was a rhetorical question. I doubted anyone knew why there were so many of either the gnomes or the wooden people.

We sat and stared at the gathering in Adele's front yard, taking it all in. I wondered if this had been a collection that had grown over the years, or if she one day decided she needed a small army of gnomes in her front yard. I also wondered what the neighbors thought of it.

"Do you think it's safe to go in?" Mom asked after a minute.

"I hope so," I said and opened my car door. I tried to get a hold of myself as I walked up the sidewalk and up the front steps. On the front porch, there were at least twenty more gnomes strategically placed in every nook and cranny.

I turned and watched as my mother slowly made her way up the porch steps, the plate of cupcakes in her hands forgotten. "I wonder how this happened?" she whispered to me.

I turned and knocked on the front door. "Quit staring," I whispered back.

When Adele opened the door, her eyes widened. "Oh hello, Rainey and Mary Ann. How nice of you to stop by."

I smiled. "Hello, Adele," I said. "We just wanted to stop by and tell you how sorry we were to hear about Arnold. He will be greatly missed."

"That's sweet of you to come by and say that," she said. "Would you like to come in?"

I nodded. "We would, thank you," I said and followed her into the house. When I glanced over my shoulder, I realized Mom wasn't behind me and I turned back and gave her a thump on the arm so she would quit staring at the gnomes. We headed back inside, following Adele into the living room.

If Mom thought the outside was something, she hadn't seen anything yet. Inside Adele's living room there was a life-sized oak tree painted on one wall. Affixed to the branches of the oak tree were sparkling fairies that had been either hand-painted into the tree or glued on. Some of them had gossamer fabric wings and plastic jewels for eyes and in their hair. We stopped and stared. There wasn't anything else we could do.

After a moment, I looked at Adele and smiled. I was pretty sure the dazed look on my face was evident. "My, what a lovely living room you have," I said looking around. There were ceramic and plush frogs placed all over the room as well as large ceramic mushrooms. Then I took in the deer and chipmunks. Every inch of the room was filled with either ceramic or plush woodland creatures. It made me dizzy trying to take it all in.

"Thank you, Rainey," Adele said and offered us a seat on the sofa. "It's my pride and joy. When I was a child, I always loved fairy tales and stories about animals, and I decided that when I grew up, I would have the home of my dreams. And well, this is it," she said and chuckled. "I bet you've never seen another one like it."

I nodded slowly and elbowed Mom. "I've never seen anything like it," I confirmed.

Mom looked at Adele and smiled. "Rainey made you some cupcakes," she said and set the plate on the coffee table. "I haven't tasted one yet, but they smell wonderful."

Adele wore her hair in a short blond bob and she pushed a lock of it back behind her ear. "Oh my, Rainey," she said. "That was so sweet of you. Arnold would have loved to have had one of these. He loved sweets, and he always told me how wonderful your cooking was. Whenever he got a chance to taste something you made, he raved about it."

That made me sad. Why hadn't I offered Arnold more than just the cupcake yesterday morning? I had occasionally given him something I had made, but I realized too late that it hadn't been often.

"Well, Arnold was always so sweet. He always had a kind word for everyone," I said.

She nodded and her lip trembled. "I just can't get over the fact that he's gone. Who would kill my Arnold?" Tears sprang to her eyes, and she brushed them away with her fingertips.

I shook my head. "I have no idea, but I know Cade is going to find the killer. They won't get away with it."

Mom still had her eyes on the decor of the living room. "Where did you find all of these—lovely things?" she asked.

Adele chuckled. "Oh, they're just items I picked up here and there. Now that we've got the Internet, it's so much easier to find unusual things. Before, I used to just look at little shops when we would travel and pick up an item or two, but now you can get things like this practically anywhere."

"Aren't we lucky?" Mom said.

Adele nodded. "We are. But I guess Arnold's luck ran out," she said and sighed. "It's still such a shock. I can't imagine what my life will be like without him. I guess it will be empty, if you want to know the truth. We always called ourselves the two musketeers. Both for one, one for both."

"I'm so sorry," I said again for something to say. I was trying hard not to stare at everything, but I had just caught sight of a smaller tree on the credenza that had flashing fireflies. I turned toward her and away from the tree. "Did Arnold ever mention anything that may have concerned you? Had he ever mentioned he was having trouble on one of his mail routes?"

She shook her head. "No, everyone loved Arnold. Well, I guess not everyone, because someone killed him. But I'll tell you ladies something," she said quietly. "If I had to guess who might have hurt Arnold, I would have to say it might have been his mother."

My eyes widened. "His mother?"

She nodded. "Oh, I'm probably just jumping to conclusions, but, his mother is something else. She always complained about poor Arnold. It seemed like he was never good enough for her."

I knew Margaret Singer and I couldn't imagine her killing her son. "Do you really think it's possible that she could kill him?"

She looked uncertain for a moment. "She was always resentful of Arnold. When she married his father, he didn't want any children. But then Margaret got pregnant with Arnold. It seemed he was very serious about not having any children because she said he told her that if she didn't put Arnold up for adoption, he would leave her. When she refused, he did just what he said he would do."

"He left her because she had a baby? His baby?" I asked incredulously.

She nodded. "He said he wanted nothing to do with a kid. He apparently had dreams of traveling the country and a kid would hold him back."

"Did he ever meet Arnold? I mean, did he leave before he was born?"

"He stayed until Arnold was three months old. Margaret said she begged and begged him to stay with her, but he wouldn't do it. He left and never looked back. Never paid a dime of child support, either. It was a classic case of a man that didn't want to be tied down. And because of that, she always resented Arnold. She always had to work to support him."

I couldn't see where it was Arnold's fault that his mother had to work to support him. Arnold hadn't chosen to be born, after all.

"But that was a long time ago," Mom said. "Why would she kill him now?"

"You don't know Margaret. Oh sure, you might know her on the surface, but what you don't know is how bitter she really is beneath it all. When Arnold and I got married, she insisted that we give her a grandbaby. And we always thought that we would, but it never happened. She thought we were holding out on her. I guess she wanted a baby that she didn't actually have to support or raise and because we couldn't have one, it just added to her resentment of Arnold," Adele said. "I guess you think I'm terrible, don't you? Here I am saying terrible things about Arnold's poor elderly mother, but I just can't get some things that she has said out of my mind."

"How does an elderly woman kill her son? Or anyone, for that matter," Mom pointed out. "Margaret Singer doesn't appear to me to be somebody that packs a pistol."

"That's what I'm saying about you not really knowing Margaret. She does have a gun. In fact, she has several. She's a member of the gun club. Of course, I could be jumping to conclusions. I really hope she didn't kill him. It would make it even more tragic."

I glanced at my mother. She looked as shocked by what Adele was saying as I felt. "I guess we don't know Margaret as well as we thought," Mom said skeptically.

I was surprised by everything Adele was saying. I felt terrible that both Adele and Margaret had lost someone they loved, and in spite of what she said about Margaret, I was sure she had to have loved her son.

Chapter Six

I COULDN'T IMAGINE Margaret Singer murdering her son. Margaret was a sweet woman that closely resembled her son in looks. Or I guess it's more correct to say that her son resembled her. She had short black hair that was quickly turning to silver, was portly, and was as pink skinned as they came. The idea of her killing her only child was disturbing, to say the least.

I had a part-time job at the local newspaper as well as the part-time job at Sam's Diner, and when I had finished up work at both places the following day, I drove over to see Margaret. I had made her some of the lemon cupcakes like the ones I had brought to Adele. I hoped she didn't mention it to Adele, because I would hate to start some sort of family war over who got lemon cupcakes first. Apparently there was already bad blood between the two of them and I didn't want to add to it.

Margaret answered the door, and I gave her a sympathetic smile. "Hello Margaret," I said. "I just wanted to stop by and tell you how sorry I was to hear about Arnold."

She gave me a smile, her full cheeks turning pink with the effort. "That's sweet of you, Rainey. Won't you come in?"

I followed her into her house and was relieved to see that her living room looked quite normal. For a moment I had wondered if she enjoyed decorating her home similarly to the way Adele did. The stately beige sofa that she had in the living room was a nice reprieve from Adele's busy living room.

"I tell you, Rainey," she said. "I don't know what I'm going to do. I just can't get over the fact that Arnold's gone."

"I can't believe it either," I said, and then remembered the plate of cupcakes in my hand. "I made you some lemon cupcakes. I'm sorry, I know it isn't much, but I thought I'd bring them by."

She smiled again. "That's so sweet of you, Rainey. You and your sister and mother are always so kind, and I do love sweets. I think Arnold got that from me," she said and chuckled. "He never could get enough cookies and cakes when he was a child, and I guess he never changed."

"I love my sweets, too," I said. "Margaret, I think we're all just in shock about what happened. Do you have any idea what might have happened Arnold?"

She shook her head slowly. "I really don't know. My boy was always so sweet. I can't imagine anyone wanting to kill him. Every time I went to the grocery store or any place else here in Sparrow, people were always stopping me and telling me how much they enjoyed having him as their mailman."

"He was so reliable and very punctual," I agreed. "Mom was just saying how much she appreciated the fact that when she had a package, he would bring it to the front door instead of just leaving a call tag." I couldn't think of one person that would want Arnold dead, but obviously someone did. And that meant that someone somewhere had to know something about Arnold's death.

"He was always so thoughtful that way. I never had a bit of trouble with him when he was growing up. All these other mothers always complained about their children, how they got into trouble. But even when Arnold was a teenager, he always minded me and was home on time."

I couldn't imagine Arnold ever having a rebellious streak in him. "I'm just so sorry this happened," I said.

She nodded and was quiet a moment, gazing at the plate of cupcakes I had set on the coffee table. Then she looked up at me and there were tears in her eyes. "There's only one person that might have had something to do with it. I say might have because I really hate pointing my finger at anyone. Especially for a crime as terrible as murder."

I nodded. "I know exactly what you're saying. It's such a terrible crime that you can't imagine anyone actually carrying it out and you hate to point at the wrong person."

"Yes, that's exactly right," she said quietly. "But if I had to point a finger at anyone, I would say it was Alice Garber."

I was shocked to hear her say Alice's name. "Alice Garber? You mean my mother's neighbor?"

She nodded again. "Yes, that Alice Garber is a strange bird. Arnold tried to do her a favor a few months ago, and she was so unthankful. She resented him for it and called him terrible names."

I sat up on the edge of my seat. Now we were getting somewhere. "What kind of favor?"

"Her refrigerator had gone out, and I had an old one I wasn't going to use anymore, so Arnold sold it to her for a hundred dollars. That was a steal, to tell you the truth, because that refrigerator worked perfectly. She should have been delighted with it, especially since she got such a good deal."

"Why did she complain about it?" I asked.

"She said it didn't work, but I know it worked perfectly well. I had only had it for eight years and it ran wonderfully. But she said that after Arnold delivered the refrigerator, it only lasted three weeks before it broke down. I can't help it if a refrigerator decides it isn't going to work anymore. When it was in my home, it did work and how am I to know whether she might have abused it in some way?"

I wasn't sure what to say about this. How would Alice have abused a refrigerator in three weeks? This wasn't what I was expecting when she said that there was a problem between Alice and Arnold.

"What did Arnold tell her when she complained about it?" I might not have wanted to know exactly what he told her. I couldn't imagine anyone killing someone over a refrigerator.

"He told her it worked fine at my house, and there wasn't anything he could do about it. And it did work fine. Do you want to know how sweet my Arnold was? Well," she continued before I could answer. "He bought me a brand-new refrigerator for Christmas. He bought it at the beginning of December so I could enjoy it throughout the holidays. It even has an icemaker and water right in the door. It's stainless steel and is the prettiest thing you've ever seen. Would you like to see it?"

I closed my mouth, which had apparently dropped open at some point during the conversation without my noticing. "Sure," I said. "I'd love to see it." What else could I say?

I followed her into the kitchen and sure enough, it was as pretty as could be. It also looked large and very expensive.

"See?" she said, holding one hand out toward it.

"It sure is pretty," I agreed. "It's very nice. But tell me, Margaret, do you really think Alice would kill over a refrigerator?" It made me wonder why Alice hadn't brought up the refrigerator when Cade and I spoke with her.

She nodded. "I do believe she would. That woman is crazy. I don't know what's going on with her, but it seems like every time I see her she gets worse and worse."

I couldn't exactly argue with her. After the conversation Cade and I had had with her a couple of days earlier, I still felt there might be something not quite right with her. "Some people do get excited about things, don't they? It's just a refrigerator, after all." I didn't want to start more trouble between the two of them, so I decided to stay neutral.

"You don't know the half of it," she said, shaking her head sadly.

"Margaret, I don't remember ever hearing anything about Arnold's father. Will he be coming to the funeral?" I had to know her side of things.

Her eyes went wide. "No. I haven't heard from him since Arnold was a baby. He wasn't the fatherly sort if you want to know the truth."

"I'm sorry to hear that," I said. "Raising a child on your own must have been difficult."

She nodded. "Especially back then. There weren't as many programs and benefits for single mothers as there are now. But, we got along. My mother helped us out where she could and would mind Arnold while I worked down at the old shirt factory. I think that was gone before you were even born, but that was where I worked. It was hard work and didn't pay much, but we managed."

I nodded. "And I know Arnold loved you for it. He always talked about you and what a wonderful mother you were."

Tears sprang to her eyes again. "He was the best son a mother could ever ask for. But that wife of his, she's something else." She shook her head. "She refused to give him children. He wanted them so badly, and she said she wasn't going to ruin her figure over babies. And just between you and me, that wasn't what ruined her figure."

I suppressed a smile and tried to think of something to say to that. "That's a shame that she didn't want children if he wanted them."

She nodded. "I knew exactly how he felt, being married to the man I was married to."

"Well Margaret, I probably should get going. If you can think of anything else, you'll be sure and let Detective Starkey know, won't you?"

"I certainly will. Aren't you dating the detective?"

I nodded. "I am. And I know he's going to find Arnold's killer as soon as possible."

"He seems like a lovely man," she said and followed me to the front door. "Tell your mother and sister I said hello."

"I will, Margaret. And if you need anything else, don't you hesitate to give me a call."

"Thank you dear," she said. She stood on the porch and watched as I got into my car. If Margaret had killed her son, she was a great actress.

Chapter Seven

I WASN'T SURE WHAT to make of Arnold Singer's murder. How could someone as meek and unassuming be murdered like that? Unless Arnold had led some kind of weird double life, there couldn't possibly be a reason someone thought he needed to die. The idea that perhaps he had been shot accidentally had crossed my mind. I supposed it was possible that someone was aiming at somebody else and accidentally shot Arnold. But even that seemed far-fetched.

"What kind of cupcakes are those?" Luanne asked me. She was peering over my shoulder as I was putting cupcakes into the display case.

"They're turtle cupcakes," I said. "Ron gave me the idea for them and I think they turned out pretty well. At the bottom of each one is a whole pecan covered in caramel."

Luanne made a face. "There are turtles in there? I've heard of turtle soup, but I've never heard of turtle cupcakes. I don't think I want one."

I turned to look at her. I could roll my eyes or say something sarcastic, but Luanne was an airhead. It didn't surprise me that she thought I would put real turtles in the cupcakes. Okay, maybe it surprised me a little. "Luanne, have you never heard of chocolate turtles? It has caramel, chocolate, and a large pecan."

A light went off, and she smiled. "Oh yes," she said. "I do know about chocolate turtles. It's one of my favorite candies."

I looked at her for a moment. "You're more than welcome to try one out," I said. "I frosted them with caramel frosting. Beneath the caramel frosting is a thin layer of chocolate icing and the cake itself is chocolate."

"That sounds really good," she said. "I think I'm going to have to have one."

She picked up one of the cupcakes from the plate and took a bite. Her eyes got big. "That's really good, Rainey," she said, nodding. "You should make cupcakes for a living."

I chuckled. "Do you think so?"

She nodded. "I really do think so. You have a real gift for making cupcakes."

"Thank you, Luanne, that's very sweet of you." I headed back to the kitchen with the rest of the cupcakes. "Okay Ron," I said. "I made your turtle cupcakes. You better grab one while they're here because I think they're going to go fast."

Ron turned around, his eyes big. "You made turtle cupcakes? For me?"

"I sure did," I said, and brought the plate of cupcakes over to where he stood in front of the sink. "They were a great idea."

"You're the best, Rainey!" He wiped his hands on a dish towel and took one of the cupcakes.

Sam turned and looked at me with a grin. "Rainey, the fact that you brought cupcakes is the best news I've heard all day.

Not that I've heard any bad news, but it's still the best news I've heard today."

I chuckled. "I'm glad I brought a little sunshine into your day."

I was working the lunch shift at Sam's, and there were a handful of customers out front. We had had another break in the weather that had gone on longer than we had expected and that was good for business. I was hoping to sell enough cupcakes to make another batch of them. As long as no one was spreading the news that we were giving away free cupcakes, I thought it wouldn't be a problem.

"You did bring some sunshine into my day," Sam said, as I held the plate out to him. "Wow, these look really good."

"Enjoy," I said. "It looks like we've got more customers out there than we've had in a while and it isn't even 11:30 yet. I hope this continues."

"You and me both," he said. "Things have been slow around here for too long. Maybe next time you can make some Boston cream cupcakes."

"That's not a bad idea," I said. "I love Boston cream pie and I'm sure cupcakes would be great, too."

"Rainey, this is wonderful," Ron said around the cupcake in his mouth. "You're my new best friend."

"Thanks," I said and laughed. "I better go back out front and see if Luanne needs some help with the customers."

I went out to the dining room just as my friend, Agatha Broome, walked through the door. She stopped and grinned at me. "Good morning, Rainey," she said cheerily. "Isn't it lovely today? The sun is shining, and the snow is melting and it's having a most happy effect on my mood."

"It is nice, isn't it?" I said. "Would you like a booth?"

She nodded. "That would be wonderful."

I picked up a menu from the hostess station and led her back to a booth in my section. "Here you go," I said. "Would you like something to drink?"

She removed the black leather gloves she wore and laid them on the table. "I think I'd like a cup of hot tea, please. And I think I want some clam chowder. It's still cold out and it will warm me right up."

"Clam chowder it is," I said. "I'll get you the tea, and if you're in the mood for something sweet, I made some turtle cupcakes. I think they turned out pretty well, but they might be a bit too sweet, so I'd appreciate it if you'd give them a try to let me know how they are."

Her eyes lit up. "If you give me a turtle cupcake, I'll give you any information you want." She laughed.

"I'll be right back with everything," I said.

I headed back to the kitchen to put the order ticket up on the order holder for Sam to see and then went to get the clam chowder for Agatha.

"Clam chowder," I told him. "I'll get it."

"Clam chowder," Sam repeated. "Still a bestseller."

"Say, Rainey," Ron said from his place by the sink. "I heard about that mailman being shot the other day. Seems a shame."

I nodded. "Isn't it though? I just hate that it was Arnold Singer. He was a nice guy."

He nodded. "I liked him real well. I only saw him when he brought the mail here to the diner, but still. It's a shame he was murdered."

I lifted one eyebrow as I held the bowl of clam chowder I was filling. "You don't happen to know anything, do you? Is anyone around town talking about the murder?"

He shook his head. "Lots of people are talking, but no one seems to know anything."

"Sam? What about you?" I asked.

He flipped a burger on the grill. "I wish I did. Whoever killed Arnold needs to be put away for a very long time."

I finished filling the bowl with clam chowder and grabbed some crackers and put them on a tray. Next, I made some hot tea for Agatha. Agatha was a British transplant, and she owned the British Tea and Coffee Company. She would occasionally drink iced tea in the summer, but she preferred her tea hot. I grabbed an English breakfast tea bag and headed back to her booth, stopping to pick up one of the cupcakes for her.

"Here we are," I said, setting the tray down on her table. I moved everything from the tray to the table in front of her. "Is there anything else I can get you?"

Her eyes went to the cupcake. "Rainey, that looks delicious. And I know it won't disappoint. I think I've probably got everything, thank you," she said and then looked up at me. "So tell me the news about Arnold Singer. I know Cade is working on the case, but does he know anything yet?"

"If he knows anything specific, he hasn't told me. You know how he is. He keeps some of what he knows to himself," I said. "Have you heard anything going around town?"

She thought about this a moment. "I'll tell you something. It wasn't two weeks ago I saw him and Alice Garber arguing at the drug store. I was really surprised because neither of those two seems like the type that would raise their voices and argue right out there in public. They probably wouldn't raise their voices even in private."

"They argued in public?"

She nodded. "They were out in the parking lot, and I heard Arnold say that something wasn't his fault. I didn't hear what that something was, but he was angry. You know how pink skinned he was, well his face was just bright red, so whatever they were discussing—it made him very angry."

"Did you hear what Alice said after that?" I asked glancing over my shoulder to make sure no one was close enough to hear our conversation.

She nodded. "Alice said she wouldn't tolerate that kind of behavior, but that was all I really heard. They were too far away for me to hear much more and there was the sound of traffic on the nearby street that blocked a lot of it out."

"I wonder what they were arguing about," I said. Margaret had said Alice was angry about the refrigerator but was that something she'd argue about in public? Like Agatha said, I wouldn't have expected either of them to behave that way. They were both quiet people.

She shrugged. "I have no idea, but you know Alice seems to be getting odder by the day. I don't know what's going on with her. She came into the coffee shop a few weeks ago and acted as if she was afraid to approach the front counter to place an order. I asked her what she wanted, and she finally walked up and ordered a cappuccino and then left right away."

What Agatha was saying made me wonder even more about Alice. Was she really beginning to lose her mind or was it an act, like my mother suggested? I didn't know, but I was going to let Cade know what Agatha had said about the argument between her and Arnold.

Chapter Eight

I WAS MAKING DINNER at my mother's house that evening when I saw Cade pull up next door at Alice Garber's house. "I'll be back in a few minutes, Mom," I said and headed out the front door before she could ask me where I was going. Cade was going to talk to Alice about Arnold's murder, and I didn't want to miss a thing.

He turned and looked at me as I walked across Mom's soggy yard. There was still snow on the ground, but it was melting fast. He stopped and narrowed his eyes at me. "What a surprise, seeing you here."

"Somehow I don't think it's that much of a surprise," I said. "So you're going to talk to Alice about the murder, right? I mean that's why you're here, right?"

He rolled his eyes. "It's almost like you read my mind."

When I got to him, I stood upon to tiptoe and gave him a kiss. "You're so smart," I said. "Let me assist you. You know she can be odd, and you might scare her."

"Yes, I'm such a scary man," he said with a chuckle, and we headed up the walk. When we got to the door, he knocked, and we waited for Alice to answer it.

This time the door swung open quickly, and I jumped a little. Alice looked from me to Cade, her eyes narrowed in suspicion.

"Good evening, Alice," Cade said. "May we have a few minutes of your time?"

Alice squinted her eyes tighter at him and then looked at me again. "What for?"

"Alice, do you remember Detective Cade Starkey?" I asked her.

She nodded. "Of course I do. Why wouldn't I remember him?" She blinked and looked from him to me and back.

I sighed. Alice was going to be difficult. "I just wanted to make sure," I said glancing at Cade.

Alice didn't say anything else but stared at both of us, looking from one to the other again and I wondered if we would be allowed inside the house.

"May we come in for a moment?" Cade repeated after a few more moments.

"Sure, why not?" she said and swung the door wide open, turned, and headed back inside.

Cade and I looked at one another before following her into the house. It had been several years since I had been inside of Alice's house, and I had a feeling things might not be the same as I remembered.

When we walked into the living room, I saw that I was right. The only furniture in the room was one straight-backed chair against the far wall. Alice went to it and sat down folding her arms across herself and looking at us, waiting.

"Well? What do you want?" she finally asked as we took in the bare room.

"Alice," I said looking around the room. "What happened to all of your furniture? And it's awfully cold in here. Shouldn't you turn up the heat?"

"If you want heat, you can go home and use your own," she said with a curt nod of her head. "I sold all my furniture."

Alarm bells went off in my head. What on earth was wrong with Alice? "You sold it? Why did you sell it?"

"So I can pay the mortgage. Why else would I sell it?" she asked, looking at me evenly.

"Alice," Cade said slowly. "It's very cold in here. I really think you should turn the heat up. For yourself, not for us." I gave Cade a sideways glance. If he was going to get anything out of her regarding the murder, he had better get asking.

"Do you know how much it costs to heat a big house like this? I can't afford that," she said firmly. Alice was dressed in a sweatshirt and wore a hot pink scarf around her neck. Her feet were clad in socks and slippers and she wore a knit hat with earmuffs. If this was the only way for her to stay warm, it made me sad.

"Mrs. Garber," Cade said, exasperation in his voice. "Do you remember hearing or seeing anything unusual the morning that Arnold Singer died?"

She thought about it a moment. "No, I don't recall seeing or hearing anything unusual. Why do you ask?"

"Because we're trying to figure out what happened," he said. "You didn't see anybody driving through the neighborhood? Anyone that seemed suspicious?"

She shook her head. "No. But if you want to know who killed Arnold Singer, you want to look at his Momma. Because that woman is evil, and she did it."

I was surprised to hear her say she thought Margaret Singer had killed Arnold. "Why would you think Margaret killed Arnold?" I asked. I couldn't wait for Cade to get the question out, so I helped him and asked it myself.

"I told you. That woman is evil. Anyone can see that. Why, anyone that would sell an elderly woman like myself a defective refrigerator, knowing that I had no extra money to spare, is evil."

I glanced at Cade again. I had already told him what Margaret had said about the refrigerator and that she suspected Alice of killing her son.

"The fact that she sold you a defective refrigerator isn't reason enough to suspect her of killing her own son," Cade pointed out dryly. "Do you have an actual reason why you think that Margaret might kill her son?"

She looked at him, narrowing her eyes. "You don't have to believe me if you don't want to. But I know that woman. She always said terrible things about her son. We played bridge once a month, and I overheard her telling people that he was nothing but a burden to her. I think she finally got tired of it all and killed him."

What Margaret was saying didn't make a lot of sense and with the missing furniture and the freezing cold room, I had to wonder if she even knew what she was saying. I really needed to speak to her kids about her.

"Alice, how was your relationship with Arnold?" Cade asked her.

She gasped, placing a hand on her chest. "My relationship? Why would you think I had a relationship with him? He was my mailman. That was all he was. Why would you ask me that?"

"You admitted that you have problems with Margaret because of the sale of a defective refrigerator. Did you also have issues with Arnold?" Cade asked.

Her lips puckered together, and she made a snorting sound. "That Arnold Singer was just like his mother! He knew that the refrigerator didn't work and yet he sold it to me. Why would he do something like that? He knew how poor I am. He knew I lived on a fixed income, and yet he sold me something he knew wasn't going to work," she seethed.

"So you did have problems with Arnold," Cade said, making a note in his notebook. "Did you see Arnold the morning he died?"

"Of course I saw him. He was leaning over the steering wheel of his mail truck." She sighed. "You ask too many silly questions."

Cade looked at her suspiciously. "When did you see him slumped over the steering wheel of his mail truck?"

"I just told you. The morning that he died."

Cade took a deep breath before continuing. "At what time of the morning did you see him slumped over the steering wheel of his mail truck?" Cade was getting annoyed, and I didn't blame him. Alice seemed to be trying to avoid his questions, and I wondered if my mother was right. Was she doing this for attention?

She shrugged. "When he was dead."

"Mrs. Garber," Cade said evenly. "Did you see him slumped over the steering wheel of the mail truck before the police arrived?"

She nodded. "Of course I did."

"Then why didn't you call the police?" he said, unable to keep the anger out of his voice. Alice's avoidance of his questions was getting to him. "Your neighbor called the police."

She shrugged. "I knew somebody would call."

My job dropped open. Alice had clearly walked up to Arnold's mail truck, looked in, and then turned around and went back to her house without calling the police.

"That's not a reasonable thing to do, Mrs. Garber," Cade pointed out. "Did it occur to you that he might still be alive and in need of medical attention?"

She shrugged again. "He didn't appear to be alive. What good would medical attention do him? Besides, the police showed up just a few minutes later."

"Mrs. Garber," Cade said evenly. "Did you shoot Arnold Singer?"

Her eyes went wide. "Of course not! I've never killed anyone in my life."

Cade studied her for a moment. "Mrs. Garber," he said. "If you had anything to do with Arnold's murder, it would be best if you came clean and told me now."

She shook her head. "You're crazy. I never did a thing. I don't have it in me to kill anyone. How can you come in here and accuse me of such a thing?"

I was just as shocked by Alice's admission that she had seen Arnold's body and done nothing about it as Cade was. I still had trouble believing she could actually kill anyone, crazy or not. But I wasn't completely sold on the fact that she might be crazy.

"Mrs. Garber, I'll be in touch." With that Cade turned and headed for the front door.

"Alice, you really do need to turn the heat up. It's too cold outside, and it's even colder inside. I don't want to see you freeze," I said.

"I'll turn the heat on when I get free heat," she said with finality.

I stared at her for a moment and then I turned and followed Cade out. I was going to ask my mother to check up on her. Maybe she could tell if Alice needed more help. In the meantime, I was going to speak to her children and see if they had noticed any strange behavior.

When I caught up to Cade I said, "what do you think of that?"

"I'm not sure what to make of it. I'd like to bring her in for further questioning, but something tells me I wouldn't get very far with it. I'll do some more investigating and see what else I can come up with. In the meantime, I'll keep an eye on her. Maybe your Mom can talk to her and see if she can find out anything."

"I'll have her do that. I'll also speak to her kids," I said. "I just can't imagine that she doesn't have enough money to turn the heat on or that she needs to sell her furniture to pay the mortgage."

"One thing's for certain," he said. "That Alice is a strange character."

He could say that again. If she had killed Arnold, I wasn't sure she had done it with a sound mind.

Chapter Nine

I LOOKED UP AS KATE Janz walked through the diner's door. We had had a different mail carrier every day since Arnold's death and I supposed it would be a temporary situation until they found someone to fill Arnold's route.

I was wiping down the front counter and I smiled. "Hi Kate," I said. "It sure is gloomy out this morning." The weather had turned cold again, and it was snowing outside.

"It sure is, but you know the mail carrier's motto; neither snow, nor rain, nor heat, nor gloom of night stays these couriers from the swift completion of their appointed rounds." She nodded. "We aim to please."

I grinned. "That's what I like to hear. Commitment. How are you this morning?"

She grinned, a handful of mail in one hand. "I'm doing as fine as I could possibly be." She laughed. "I am the happy possessor of a brand-new mail route and a nice warm mail truck that has a heater in it."

"Oh? Does that mean you're going to be our regular mail carrier?" I asked.

She nodded. "It sure does. I can hardly believe my luck. And I can hardly believe how warm my new mail truck is. It sure does make me appreciate it with the snow falling out there."

"Didn't your old mail truck have a heater?" I asked. And for a moment, I wondered if she had the same mail truck that Arnold had died in. But that was silly. I was sure the police had that truck in evidence.

"Mail truck?" She laughed again. "I never had a mail truck. I had to walk my route. I can't tell you how miserable that was in the snow. Plus, I always had to be looking over my shoulder to make sure there wasn't a dog chasing after me." She shook her head. "I tell you, Arnold's route was one of the best there is in Sparrow. Everyone wanted it. He was always getting treats from his customers and fudge at Christmas time. You know what I got at Christmas from my customers?"

"No, what?"

"A great big fat nothing! Everyone envied Arnold."

"Really? I had no idea," I said. I couldn't imagine walking a mail route in the snow and while I knew it was done, I had never stopped to think about how difficult that would be.

She nodded. "Yep. Arnold had the cream of the crop when it came to mail routes."

I didn't know there was such a thing as a cream of the crop of mail routes. You learn something new every day. "Well it will be nice getting to see you every day, then."

"I can hardly wait. Arnold used to brag on all the baked goods he used to get from you when he came in to deliver the mail." She looked at me, grinning with expectation.

That was news to me. Sure, occasionally I gave him something like on the morning of the day that he died, but it hadn't happened that often. "Well, I'm glad he enjoyed what I made. Did you see him the morning he died? I gave him a chocolate cherry cupcake." I knew Arnold had told a lot of people about free cupcakes that day, but I hadn't seen Kate come in to ask for one.

"Oh sure," she said. "I saw him that morning when we both came to work. He said he was so glad he didn't have to walk his route. That was like him, you know. He was always rubbing it in that he had a nice warm mail truck. I must've missed out on the cupcakes."

"I didn't know that about him," I said taking this in. Maybe Arnold wasn't quite as sweet as I had taken him to be and he had provoked the wrong person.

"I bet there was a lot you didn't know about Arnold Singer," she said conspiratorially. "He was the postmaster's pet if you want to know the truth. He was always hanging around her and telling her how pretty she was. Please! Everyone knows Heidi Griggs isn't pretty."

I wasn't sure what to say to that. Kate looked like she was in her early 40s and she never wore makeup. She had what could best be described as a brawny physique, if women had brawny physiques, that is.

"Well," I said trying to come up with something else to say. "It sure was a shame to hear about Arnold. I can't understand who would want to hurt him."

She narrowed her eyes at me. "Oh? Can't you?"

I wasn't sure if this was meant to hint at something or not. "No, I really can't. Can you?"

"Well, if I had to take a guess," she said looking over her shoulder and then back at me. She still had our mail in her hand, and she slapped it against her free hand. "It wouldn't surprise me one bit if his wife killed him. I wouldn't blame her for doing it either, if you want to know the truth."

I was surprised at this. "Why would you say that?"

"Because I don't think she really liked him very much. We had a company Christmas party in December, and she came with him. They had an argument right there in front of everyone. I couldn't believe it, and Heidi Griggs tried to step in the middle of it and make them stop. Adele told her that she better get out of her face or she would be sorry. If you ask me, it wouldn't surprise me one bit if Adele had been drinking."

Hearing that our county librarian might have been drunk at a Christmas party was a little surprising to me. It shouldn't have been, I suppose, but Adele didn't seem the type to drink, what with all of her fairies and frogs.

"What did they argue about?"

She shrugged. "I only heard part of it, but she was mad about something he bought his mother. I don't know what it was, but it made her hot. She said that was her money, and he didn't have a right to spend it without asking her."

I wasn't sure if she was referring to the refrigerator that he had given Margaret or not, but it had looked expensive. "A lot of couples argue. It doesn't mean that one would kill the other." Did Kate know more, or was she just enjoying gossiping about Arnold?

"I suppose not," she said agreeing with me. "But Adele just has this way about her. She seemed completely disgusted with him and it wasn't the first time I've seen her act that way. She's always looking down on people she thinks are beneath her. Arnold said she wanted a baby and he couldn't give her one. If you ask me, I think she's been resentful about it ever since they found out."

"Well, I guess I can see where someone might be very disappointed if they wanted to have children and couldn't, but I can't imagine one person in the marriage blaming the other. At least not to the point where one might kill the other. There's something called divorce, after all."

"I'm telling you, Rainey," she said, nodding. "Adele had something to do with Arnold's murder. But I guess it doesn't mean anything to me. I'm just thrilled that I've got his mail route now." She peered over my shoulder and saw the display plate of cupcakes. "Are those cupcakes?"

"Why don't I take that mail from you?" I said, changing the subject. "I'm sure Sam has been expecting something." I was a little disgusted by her glee at getting Arnold's mail route as a result of his death.

"Oh sure." She handed me the stack of mail and I began looking through it and headed back behind the counter to take it to Sam. "Oh, Rainey?"

I turned back. "Yes?"

"What about those cupcakes?" she asked and pointed to the display stand.

"Oh, those are cupcakes I'm trying out for my new cookbook. They're a dollar each."

A look of disappointment crossed her face. "A dollar? Arnold said that you gave him cookies and cupcakes all the time."

I didn't know if Arnold had really said that, or if she was just hoping I'd give her one. "He did? I wonder why he would say that? No, I'm selling them for a dollar so I can buy more ingredients to make another batch. Would you like to buy one?"

She clenched her fists by her side and stared longingly at the cupcakes. "I guess I better not. I still have most of my mail route to complete. But maybe tomorrow if there are some left, I'll get one."

"Okay. Sounds good," I said and turned and headed back toward the kitchen. "See you tomorrow." It may have been unkind not to offer her a free cupcake, but she had gotten on my nerves with what she said about Arnold. I didn't know if it was true or not, and maybe it was unfair of me to hold it against her, but I couldn't help it. She brought it out in me.

"Mail, Sam," I said as I headed to his office.

"Yay," he said unenthusiastically. "Is that Kate Janz that brought the mail in?"

"Yup, she's our new mail carrier," I told him. "And she's darned pleased to get Arnold's route."

"I guess the mail must be delivered, regardless of whether one of their own was mowed down in the line of duty."

"Somebody's got to do it," I said and sighed. I wondered if Kate's desire for Arnold's mail route was strong enough to cause her to murder.

Chapter Ten

I LOOKED UP FROM MY computer as Karen Forrest walked out of her office. I was at my second part-time job, the Sparrow Daily News writing an article on Valentine's Day. I wasn't sure what Cade, and I were going to do for the day. He had been so wrapped up in Arnold Singer's murder case that I hadn't had a chance to ask him. I wasn't sure what I wanted to do. My relationship with Cade was mending my poor broken heart, but was I ready to do something over the top romantic for Valentine's Day? I really didn't think so.

"Good morning, Rainey," Karen said, walking up to my desk. "I heard about poor Arnold Singer. I just can't believe that someone shot him in his mail truck in the middle of the morning."

"I can't either. It shocks me that anyone can commit murder at all, but especially to carry it out in broad daylight," I said, shaking my head.

"I saw where Kate Janz took over his route," she said sitting on the edge of my desk. "Kate's nice. I don't know her very well, but she seemed very enthusiastic about inheriting the route."

I chuckled. "She did seem excited, didn't she? She stopped in at the diner yesterday morning and told me about it. She said the route was a desirable one."

"Well I had never considered one mail route to be more desirable than another one, but I guess you have to be a mail carrier to understand that. Does Cade have any idea what might have happened to Arnold?"

"It's still early in the investigation, but he's working on it," I said. "If you hear anything you think might be helpful, you'll let me know, won't you?"

She nodded. "I certainly will. Hopefully the police will get it figured out soon."

We both looked up as the front door opened and Gina Richards walked through it. I smiled at Karen, got to my feet, and went to the front counter. I wrote articles part-time, but I also worked the front counter when needed. Although ads could be placed online, many still liked to come into the office to place an ad or start a subscription. Small towns are like that.

Karen went back to her office, and I turned to Gina. "Good morning, Gina," I said. "What can I help you with?" Gina had opened the Happy Petals flower shop several months earlier. Since my mother had made mention of the fact that business had been slow, I wondered if it was the same for Gina.

"I want to run an ad in the paper for Valentine's Day. You know it's the busiest day of the year for us florists, don't you?" She grinned.

"I think I may have heard that somewhere before," I said and chuckled.

"I can hardly wait! My very first Valentine's Day as a florist. I know it's going to be absolutely wonderful," she said. Gina was lit up like a Christmas tree. It was refreshing to see someone so excited about their job, even though she was my mother's competition.

"I'm sure it will be exciting," I said and handed her the form we used for people to fill out to place an ad in the newspaper. "This winter sure has been crazy, hasn't it? It seems like we've got more snow than we normally do, other than the break in the weather earlier in the week."

"It sure has been," she said as she bent over the form to fill it out.

I didn't want to be obvious, but I really needed to know. Mom might complain about everything else, but she never complained much about her own problems, so it had been a surprise when she admitted that business hadn't been good lately.

"So, how has your first year in business been? I mean, your first few months?" I asked.

She looked up at me and beamed. "Wonderful! It has exceeded my expectations. I always knew it would be such fun to own a flower shop, but I didn't know exactly how much fun. This has probably been the best idea I've ever had in my entire life," she said and laughed. "Listen to me go on. I can't help it though, I'm excited."

"Really? Business has been that good?" I asked, hoping she didn't read into it that my mother's business wasn't good.

She nodded. "It really has been. The holidays were fantastic and I'm so excited about my business. But I'm sure you know exactly what I mean. I bet your mother's business has been booming too. Right?"

I had to bite my tongue to keep from saying what I wanted to say. Gina read right through me and knew exactly what I was asking. "Oh, of course. You know what a well-established business she has. People love her and I was just speaking to her the other day about Valentine's Day. She was so thrilled it was coming around because, like you said, it is the busiest day of the year for florists." Okay, I lied. Sue me. I wasn't going to admit to Gina that things were tough for my mother. It was temporary, and I was sure things would turn around soon.

She continued writing without comment and it made me want to say something for spite. I bit my tongue instead. When she finished, she slid the paper across the counter to me and grinned.

I looked it over. Unfortunately, it was cutesy and darling. Every woman in Sparrow would want their man to buy something from Happy Petals flower shop. I refrained from sighing and wondered why Mom hadn't been in to place an ad for her shop. Valentine's Day was three days away. She should have already done it.

I looked up and smiled at Gina. "All right then, we'll get the ad placed," I said and rang up her purchase.

"Thanks, Rainey. I know you all will do a great job on the ad." She paused a moment, then continued. "I heard there was another murder in town. It's just terrible that that kind of thing has been happening around here. Does Cade have any idea who might have done it?"

"It's still early in the investigation, but he's been hard at work on the case," I said without looking at her. I just wanted her out of the office. I needed to call Mom and ask why she hadn't placed an ad in the paper yet.

She nodded. "I heard Arnold's replacement, Kate Janz, really hated him."

I slowly looked at her. "Oh? Why would she hate him?"

"Well, you know when someone applies for a job at the post office they've got to do a lot of tests. I heard she cheated on the test and he caught her and told their supervisor."

"Why would they have hired her if she cheated on the employment test?" What she was saying really didn't make sense to me. If Kate was trying to get on at the post office, and she were caught cheating on the pre-employment exam, why would they have hired her? "Who did you hear that from?"

She shrugged and grinned. "I can't reveal my sources. See, I'm just like a reporter, you know," she said and chuckled. "I've got to keep my sources close to the vest."

It took all the strength in me not to roll my eyes at her. She thought she was being cute, but she was really just being a jerk. "Then why was she hired? If the higher-ups at the post office knew she cheated, there's no way they would have hired her. I'd talk to that source of yours if I were you. Because clearly, they don't know what they're talking about."

She shrugged and chuckled again. "You don't have to believe me if you don't want to. But I'm telling you, she really had something against Arnold. And how easy would it have been for her to slip up behind him while he was working on his mail route and shoot him?"

What she said made me stop and think. Not because I thought Kate might have snuck up behind him and shot him, because she might have. But, I had been assuming he had been shot from the front. But how would that have happened if the windshield of the mail truck wasn't broken, and it wasn't. I needed to ask Cade what he knew about that. But as for Gina's claims that Kate had been caught cheating on the pre-employment exam at the post office, I didn't buy it. She was just talking to get attention.

I shrugged and chuckled. "Well then, maybe the police need to pay you a visit. Seeing as how you have inside information that they might find interesting."

The smile left her face, and she narrowed her eyes at me. "You know what, Rainey? I was just trying to help you. And if you don't want any help, fine. I won't help you. Are we done here?"

"Oh yes," I said still smiling. "We're done here."

I was as done with Gina Richards as I could be. When her sister-in-law was murdered last year, she had been nothing but unhelpful every time I had talked to her about what might have happened to her. She was smug and snarky and I decided then that I simply didn't like her.

Cade would know more about what happened to Arnold by now. I tried not to pry information out of him, but it was hard sometimes.

Chapter Eleven

I WALKED INTO THE BRITISH Tea and Coffee company and spotted Stormy and my Mom at a corner table. I waved at them and went to the front counter to get a coffee. Agatha's latest concoction was a cherry mocha, piled high with whipped cream and a maraschino cherry on top, just in time for Valentine's Day. I had to have it. I placed my order and headed over to Mom's and Stormy's table and took a seat.

"Hi Mom, hi Stormy. What's going on with you two?" I asked as I took a sip of my coffee. Chocolatey cherry goodness assailed my taste buds, and I groaned. "This is so good."

"I know it is, isn't it?" Stormy agreed. "I got a cherry mocha, too."

"Me three," Mom said and took a sip of her drink.

"I swear Agatha makes the best coffee around. I mean sure, you could probably get a cherry mocha anywhere this time of year, but there's just something about the drinks she makes," Stormy said.

I had to agree. Agatha had a way with the brewed beverage. I looked up and saw Agatha heading toward us. She waved and grinned.

"Hello ladies," she said, taking a seat at the table. "I was wondering when the four of us were going to get together for a chat. It seems like it's been ages."

I laughed. "You always say that Agatha, but I swear we're in here several times a week to sit down and catch up."

Agatha chuckled. "Maybe so," she said. "But I work so many hours that you three are my only source of entertainment. I miss it when you all don't come around."

I nodded. "I miss it when I don't come around, too."

"We really need to get away from here and just have lunch together," Stormy suggested. "Then we won't have to worry about customers coming in and pulling you away from us, Agatha."

"That is a great idea," Agatha agreed. "We should do it. We could go shopping afterward."

"That's an even better idea," Stormy said.

I looked over at Mom. She was being unusually quiet. "Mom, how is business this week?"

She looked at me, eyes wide, then shrugged. "It's fine. It's about the same. You know how winter is. Things slow down."

"Yes, but Valentine's Day is just around the corner. Have you put an ad in the newspaper yet?" I asked.

She shook her head. "No, I must have forgotten to do that. I guess I need to get on it."

"You'd better do it quick. Today is the deadline, so when you're done here, you should stop by the newspaper and put the ad in."

She nodded but didn't look at me. "Sure, I'll do that."

Stormy and I looked at each other wide-eyed. "Mom, what's going on?" Stormy asked.

"Nothing's going on," she insisted. "It's just winter. I told you that. Things will pick up when it warms up."

"Yes, but it's nearly Valentine's Day. I would think some people would put their orders in early, don't they?" I asked.

"Oh, yes," Agatha said. "Everything we've got that's heart-shaped or cherry or strawberry flavored is flying off the shelves. I brought in a lot of Valentine's Day candy from Britain and I've nearly sold out already. Not to mention the coffee drinks that are Valentine's Day themed. I can hardly keep the cherry flavored syrup in stock."

"See?" I said to Mom. "Your business should have already picked up. Now what's going on?"

She sat back in her chair and shook her head. "It's fine. Everything is fine. I don't know why you two worry so much."

I didn't believe her. She was worried. It showed on her face and in everything she said.

"Mom, is it the new flower shop?" Stormy asked, taking a sip of her drink.

"I suppose it's taken a bit of my business," she admitted without meeting anyone's eyes. "You know how it is. When a new business comes to town, everyone wants to try it out. But they'll be back. I've been in business for more than twenty years and I know this is just a temporary lull."

I didn't like that Mom's business was suffering. I also didn't like that Mom was struggling with these things. She seemed so down and depressed. We needed to come up with a plan to help her. "If there's something that we can do to help you Mom, we're more than happy to do it."

She smiled and nodded. "Of course you are. I have the best girls in the whole world." Her voice cracked a little when she said it, and that made me feel worse.

We all looked up as Cade walked through the door and headed to our table. "Now here's what I like to see. My four favorite ladies sitting around and kicking back with a nice hot coffee." He pulled a chair over from a nearby table and sat down next to me as I scooted my chair over to give him some room.

"Mom's business is suffering," I informed him. "We need to come up with a way to help her out and get it back on track."

Mom gasped. "Rainey! Everything will be fine. I told you, everything will be just fine. It's just a temporary slowdown. It will pass."

"I'm sorry to hear that you're having trouble," Cade said. "But if it makes you feel any better, I'm going to place a great big order for flowers for a wonderful woman that I know. I haven't known her long, but I feel like I've known her my entire lifetime."

I felt myself blush. Cade could be sweet and corny when he wanted to be.

"I'm glad to hear that," Mom said, brightening. "Not just for the business, but because I'm glad the two of you are so happy together."

Mom was never the sentimental type, and this caught me by surprise. "Thanks, Mom."

"Now then, Cade," she said turning to him. "How is the investigation into Arnold's death going?" Changing the subject was her way of saying she didn't want to talk about her business troubles in front of Cade.

"It's going about as well as can be expected," he said. "We got the results back from the autopsy and he was shot with a 9mm shell. It's a fairly common bullet."

"I never did ask you," I said remembering what I had thought about the day before. "Was he shot from the front or the back? I don't remember seeing that the windshield was cracked."

"He was shot from in front, at close range, so the windshield wouldn't have been hit. We only found evidence of one bullet being shot."

"Someone just walked right up to him and shot him in the chest?" I asked. "I guess they could have had a silencer, and that's why no one heard anything."

He nodded. "They walked right up to him and shot him, and I would bet they did have a silencer. That or they got really lucky that no one heard anything."

"So he had to have known them," Stormy said. "Because he would've driven off if he had seen the gun or if he felt threatened in any way."

"That's a very good possibility," Cade said. He wasn't going into details, and I thought he must know more than he was telling us.

"But he never turned his mail truck off," I pointed out. I wanted more information, and I was going to get it if I could.

"Because he didn't want to get behind on his route. You know how he was," Mom added, sitting up in her chair. "Look at us. We're all becoming crack sleuths. Maybe we should all do this for a living. It's not like we have anything else to do with our lives."

I chuckled. "How about it, Cade? Would you like to take on three assistants?"

"What do you mean three assistants?" Agatha asked. "You mean four. I want in on the action."

Cade narrowed his eyes at me and grinned. "I don't think it's in the police department's budget to take on any assistants."

"Seriously though," I said to him. "Do you think it will be much longer before you make an arrest?"

He shrugged. "You know I can't tell you everything I know. I think I need to get a coffee."

"Oh no," Agatha said, getting to her feet. "You sit right there. I'll get you a coffee. Do you know what you want?"

"There's a great cherry mocha on the menu," I suggested.

"Sounds good to me," he said.

"I'll be right back with it." Agatha headed to the counter to make his drink.

"So, what do you two love birds have planned for Valentine's Day?" Mom asked Cade and me.

I began to shake my head and Cade reached over and put his hand on mine. "I am taking Rainey out for a wonderful dinner on Valentine's Day. He turned to me. "I hadn't gotten around to telling you yet, but I have reservations over at the Bistro Moncur in Boise. Sound good?"

I smiled. "Sounds good," I said. I hoped he wasn't going all out. I really preferred something simple, but I didn't know how to tell him in front of everyone. I would try to get him alone later and suggest that we just have a nice dinner and leave it at that. He already mentioned buying flowers, so maybe I was too late, but I hoped it wasn't.

"We'll call it a date then," he said and gave my hand a squeeze. "I can hardly wait."

I leaned over and gave him a quick kiss. "Me too."

Dating Cade had been a dream come true after a nightmare divorce, and I still had trouble believing he was mine. He had brightened up what had begun as a dreary year last year and I hoped I wouldn't do anything to ruin what we had going.

Chapter Twelve

THE DAY OF ARNOLD'S funeral dawned cold and gloomy. It was fitting weather for a funeral. Who wanted to bury someone on a bright sunny day?

Stormy and my mother and I drove over to the Baptist Church together. I wasn't sure if Cade would make it or not. The previous evening, I had asked him if he was going and he said he wasn't sure he could get away from the office. I thought going to funerals was good practice. Since the killer usually returns to the scene of the crime, I thought there was a pretty good chance they would show up to the funeral as well to make sure their handiwork had done the job and the victim really was dead.

"One thing is for sure," Mom said. "Arnold's death has been good for my business."

"Mom," I said as I pulled into the parking lot. "That isn't appropriate. Please tell me you won't say something like that to anyone at the funeral."

She snorted. "Why would you think I would do that? I'm not a monster."

"Sorry," I said as we got out of the car. "I just don't want anyone to be more upset than they already are."

"The only people that will really be upset is Adele and Margaret. Everyone else just comes to funerals out of obligation. It's such a shame those ladies have lost someone very dear to them," Mom said sounding genuine. "And thank goodness a lot of the arrangements were bought at my shop."

I sighed. So much for sounding genuine. At least she sounded more like herself.

"There's a lot of people here," Stormy whispered.

"It doesn't surprise me. I'm sure a lot of people will miss him, and it won't be out of obligation," I said as we walked into the church. The inside of the church was nearly filled. Arnold had been a popular mailman and citizen in Sparrow, and I was glad to see the turnout. It would bring comfort to Adele and Margaret.

We sat in the back of the church so we could keep an eye on things. People milled about, talking to one another while Adele and Margaret sat on the front pew. Adele was at one end and Margaret at the other. I hated to see that, and I wished they had been able to at least put aside their differences until after the funeral. Some people took stubbornness to new heights, even at a funeral.

"If you ask me, Trish Callahan, looks mighty suspicious," Mom whispered, leaning over toward me.

Trish Callahan owned a small shoe store in the middle of town. She had short blonde hair and was in her early sixties but dressed as if she were in her twenties. She was leaning over and speaking to a woman that I recognized but couldn't come up with a name for. "Why do you think Trish Callahan is suspicious?" I whispered.

"She's a hussy," Mom said, nodding her head.

I looked at Mom. "Seriously? Who uses that word anymore?"

"I do."

I shook my head. "She probably didn't even know Arnold."

"Okay, but you mark my words," Mom said. "She's suspicious. Wouldn't surprise me a bit if Cade arrested her in the next few days."

I ignored her. Sometimes that was the only thing Stormy and I could do with our mother. But at least she was back to being herself. Maybe things had picked up at the flower shop and not just because of Arnold's funeral.

"It's nice so many people showed up today," Stormy whispered.

"I hope they have good snacks after the funeral," Mom said.

"Mom," I warned. She shrugged and turned forward as the pastor took the podium.

IT WAS A LOVELY FUNERAL, or at least it was as lovely as a funeral could be. I was thankful it was a closed casket though. I hated to look at the dead and would prefer to remember them the way I had last seen them. Occasionally Adele dabbed at her cheek with a tissue. Margaret's shoulder shook now and then, and then she would take a deep breath and get ahold of herself. It broke my heart that these two wonderful women were in such pain.

When the service was over, we made our way toward the front to pay our respects to Adele and Margaret. We waited in line while others did the same and when I finally got to Adele, she reached out and took my hand, "Rainey," she whispered. "Can I speak with you in private?"

"Sure," I said, and she pulled me over next to Arnold's casket. I was thankful once again that it was closed. "What's up?"

She turned her back to the people behind us and looked at me imploringly. "I know who the killer is."

"Who?" I asked as the line I had been in moved over to where Margaret sat to offer her their condolences.

"I've been racking my brain, and I finally came on the answer last night as I was trying to fall asleep. I'm having a terrible time sleeping without Arnold by my side," she said, shaking her head. "But it's Kate Janz."

I looked over Adele's shoulder and saw Kate with some of her coworkers in the middle of the church. None of them had made their way forward to pay their respects. Kate was laughing about something.

"Why do you say that?" I whispered.

"Well, I can't believe I completely forgot about this but," she said glancing over her shoulder again. "But she accused Arnold of sexual harassment last year. How stupid am I that I forgot about that?"

My eyebrows furrowed. "Sexual harassment? Against Arnold? Are you serious?"

She nodded. "I know how insane that sounds, and that's what I told Arnold when he told me about it." She laughed and waved away the idea. "Can you imagine it? Arnold didn't have a harassing bone of any kind in his body, and he certainly didn't have it in him to sexually harass anyone."

"What happened with the case?" I asked.

"It went on for several weeks," she said. "Kate insisted Arnold had cornered her in the mail room and made her feel uncomfortable." She made air quotes with her fingers when she said the word 'uncomfortable'. "I can't imagine anything more ridiculous."

It sounded ridiculous to me, too. Arnold was mild-mannered and unassuming, and I didn't believe for a minute that he would do something like that. "And there were no witnesses?"

She shook her head. "None. And in the end, that was finally what convinced the human resources department that nothing had happened. There was no one to back up her story, and they knew Arnold. He didn't have it in him."

"So why do you think she would kill him now if this happened last year?"

"I think she was just biding her time, waiting until the whole thing died down. She was humiliated that no one believed her." She glanced over her shoulder in Kate's direction.

It was certainly a possibility that she would be embarrassed enough to want to get back at Arnold. But a year later? "Why do you think Kate would have claimed sexual harassment to begin with?"

"Because she wanted his route. She thought Arnold had the best route in all of Sparrow. When she asked Arnold to change routes with her, he refused. He wasn't a fool, you know," she said shaking her head. "When Arnold refused, she became livid. She told him she would get back at him, and she did by trying to get him in trouble at work. I think she wanted him fired, not just reprimanded."

I glanced over at Kate again. She and the other three post office employees she was with were headed toward the back of the church without ever coming forward to speak to either Adele or Margaret. It was rude if nothing else.

"I suppose it's something Cade should look into," I agreed. "At the very least he can have a talk with her and see what he thinks."

She nodded. "That's exactly what I thought. If she had anything to do with his death, I bet she'll crack when the detective tells her he wants to interview her. You wait and see, Rainey," she said. "I really think she killed Arnold. I think she'll be the one to be arrested."

"I'll definitely mention it to him," I said, watching Kate as she left the church.

"Thanks, Rainey," she said and gave my hand a squeeze. "I better get back to greeting people. You let me know what he thinks about it."

I headed over to join Mom and Stormy as they spoke to Margaret. "Margaret," I said. "Again, I'm so sorry about Arnold." I reached out and gave her hand a squeeze.

"Thank you so much, girls," she said, including Mom and Stormy. "I appreciate you all coming out to the funeral. I still don't know what I'm going to do without my Arnold. I miss him so much."

"I'm sorry, Margaret," Stormy said. "If there's anything you need us to do for you, don't you hesitate to give us a call."

"I will," Margaret said nodding. "Thank you."

We made our way to the back of the church and then out to my car. I didn't like the fact that Kate Janz had seemed so unaffected by Arnold's death. Actually, unaffected was the wrong word for it. She was celebrating the fact that she got his mail route. I was definitely going to talk to Cade about what Adele had told me.

Chapter Thirteen

I HAD INTENDED TO TALK to Alice Garber's children about what was going on with her when Cade and I had talked to her the previous week. But time had slipped away, and I hadn't gotten around to doing it. Her daughter Jennifer worked at the grocery store and her son Jack worked at the community college in Boise. I thought Alice needed help, but I wasn't sure exactly what kind.

The day after the funeral I had to stop by the grocery store to pick up a few things when I saw Jennifer standing at the meat counter. She was on the customer side of the counter, so I figured she must have a day off. I pushed my shopping cart up to where she was.

"Good morning, Jennifer," I said. "How are you? Are you off work today?"

She turned and looked at me and smiled. "Hi Rainey," she said and nodded. "I sure am. And what do I do on my day off? I come to work. But I'm only here to pick up a few things and then I'm going to enjoy the rest of the day."

"I'm jealous you have the day off," I said. "I have to work a shift at the diner later today. Say Jennifer, how is your mother doing?"

She shrugged. "Okay, I guess. I keep meaning to go by her house and check up on her. I usually see her at least every other week if not every week, but I've been busier than usual lately, and it's been about three weeks since I saw her. Why?"

"I just wondered. I saw her last week, and to be honest, I was a little concerned. There wasn't any furniture in her house and the house was freezing cold. She said she had to sell the furniture to pay the mortgage and she couldn't afford to run the heater."

Jennifer rolled her eyes. "She told you that? Why am I not surprised? Don't believe anything she says. All the furniture is in the dining room."

I blinked in surprise. "In the dining room? Why?"

"She does this every now and then. Is just a plea for attention. She has more than enough money to make her mortgage payment and to run the heater. My mother has always had a flair for the dramatic and it's gotten worse since she's gotten older."

I was stunned at this information. "Really? Because she seemed so convincing when she said she had no money."

She shook her head. "Like I said, it's just a bid for attention. I told her that I can't come over every day like she wants, and so she'll tell other people that she's being neglected. But I promise you, my brother and I both stop in regularly."

I took this in. Alice had been in her forties when she had both her children. I could see where maybe as she was aging, and they were just beginning to live their separate, independent lives, she might feel lonely. "Maybe you should stop in again then," I suggested as kindly as I could manage. "It's really too cold for her to go without heat."

"She only does that during the day. At night she'll turn the heater on to sleep. She wears a lot of layers during the day in the hopes that somebody will stop by and feel sorry for her when they see how cold the house is." She smiled and shrugged. "We've been through this before."

I bit my lower lip, considering this. I wanted to believe that what she was saying was true, but what if Alice was truly losing her mind and her kids weren't taking it seriously? "How do you think she is mentally? Does she seem off to you?"

"She's sharp as a tack. I promise you, Rainey," she said. "The only thing my mother lacks is the ability to leave the house and spend time with people. She's kind of becoming a recluse, except when she really wants something. Then she has no problem going out and getting it."

I nodded. "Okay, then," I said. "I was just a little worried is all. I'm glad things aren't as bad as she made them seem."

She chuckled. "No, they aren't anywhere near as bad as she tries to make out that they are."

I was somewhat relieved. But I still thought it was odd that she would behave the way she had, even if it was to get attention. It also made me wonder if she really might be losing her mind, and maybe she had shot Arnold. Maybe it was an accident, and she didn't even realize what she had done.

"Well, thanks for letting me know," I said after thinking it over.

"No problem. I promise I will stop in and see her later today, but she's fine."

"That sounds good then, Jennifer," I said. "I've got to get going so I can get ready for my shift at Sam's."

"See you later, Rainey," she said and turned back to the meat case.

I pushed my shopping cart further down the meat department aisle. I was reasonably sure Jennifer was telling me the truth, but it still bothered me. Maybe she wasn't aware that her mother was losing some of her mental faculties. I bought the few items I needed from the grocery store and decided I would stop in and see how Alice was doing.

I STOPPED OFF AT ALICE'S house on my way to work. When she opened the door, she looked at me and pursed her lips. "What do you want?"

"Good morning, Alice," I said cheerily. "I just stopped by to check on you. I brought you some cookies." I had picked up the cookies at the grocery store on a whim. I didn't have time to bake her some homemade cookies, and I wasn't sure she would even notice.

She peered at the plastic clamshell box of cookies I held out to her. "Are they oatmeal raisin?"

"They sure are," I said. "I hope you like oatmeal raisin."

She gave a curt nod of her head and grabbed the cookies from me. "Want to come in? You can't stay long. I'm busy," she said and turned and went back into the house without waiting for my reply.

I followed after her. "Sure," I said. I stopped in my tracks. The foyer was warm. I followed her into the living room. There was still only one chair in the room, and she sat down in it.

"I do like cookies," she said looking over the box in her lap.

"I'm glad to hear it," I said lightly. "Alice, it's nice that this room is warm today."

"Of course it is. It's cold outside. Why wouldn't the house be warm?"

I sighed. I didn't want to go through the twenty questions routine again. "Alice, is it true your furniture is in your dining room?"

She looked at me, surprised. "You've been talking to Jennifer, haven't you?"

I grinned. "I may have. Is it true? Is your furniture in your dining room?"

She hesitated before answering. "So what if it is? I can keep my living room furniture in my dining room, can't I? It's my dining room."

"Of course you can. But why did you tell us you had to sell it in order to pay the mortgage?"

"Because I wanted to." Her chin jutted out stubbornly, but she wouldn't look at me.

"Alice, you can keep your furniture anywhere you please. Are you sure you didn't see anything the morning that Arnold Singer was murdered?"

She squinted her eyes at me. "I might have. There was a car that drove through the neighborhood that I didn't recognize."

"What kind of car?" I asked her.

"It was a dark SUV. Black, I think. I think it belonged to Margaret Singer."

I didn't think Margaret Singer owned a black SUV. The last time I had seen her in a car, she was driving a red hatchback. "Alice, do you own a gun?"

Her eyes went wide. "Of course I do! Someone broke into my house six years ago and I bought a gun so I can keep an eye on my house and the neighborhood."

"What kind of gun is it?" I asked. She was in a talking mood and I needed to get all the information that I could while she was talking.

"Oh, I forget exactly what kind of gun it is. But it takes a 9mm bullet. The man that sold it to me said to make sure I get only that kind of bullet," she said, off-handedly. "If anybody tries to rob me again, they're going to regret it. I keep a watch on your mother's house too. You would think she would thank me for that, but she never has said thank you."

9mm bullet. "I'm sure she does appreciate it. I certainly appreciate that you're watching out for her," I said. As soon as I said it, I thought better of it. She might accidentally shoot my mother. "Alice, have there been any intruders around lately?"

She shook her head. "No. None. Why?"

I shrugged. "I don't know. There was a murder here in the neighborhood and I just wondered if maybe the person who is responsible for it might have come back."

She shook her head. "No. It was Margaret Singer. Why don't you believe me? That woman is evil, and you have to keep an eye on her. She'll strike again, I tell you. Watch and see."

I wasn't sure that Margaret Singer was evil. I wasn't completely sure that she hadn't killed her son, but I still couldn't imagine her running around shooting anyone.

"I'm sure the detective will be looking into it," I said. "Do you have anything solid that makes you believe she's a killer? Something the police can look into?"

She sighed. "She's a crack shot. I've seen her down at the gun range and she never misses her mark."

The idea that Margaret Singer could be a crack shot sounded laughable to me, but Alice was as serious as could be. "You're sure of this?"

She nodded. "Of course I am. You keep an eye on that woman. She knows far more than she's letting on. She told Aggie Andrews down at the gun club that Arnold was an albatross around her neck. Said she could have done so much more with her life if he hadn't been born."

"Do you really think she said that?"

She nodded. "Of course. She's that kind of person."

I nodded. "Okay Alice," I said. "I just wanted to check in on you and see how you were doing. How *are* you doing Alice?"

"I'm doing okay. I've got cookies now, and the heat is on, and everything is okay. I do appreciate your stopping by." She said the last part quietly while looking at the cookies she held in her lap. It made me sad.

"Well, if you ever need any help moving that furniture from the dining room back into the living room, don't hesitate to let me know, okay?"

She ignored me and opened up the package of cookies and pulled one out. She looked it over carefully and then took a huge bite.

"Okay Alice," I said when she didn't answer me. "I've got to get going. I've got to get to work."

She never answered me, and I left her house. I was uncertain as to what the problem was with Alice. I hoped Jennifer might notice something different about her and if she needed some kind of help, that she would get it for her.

Chapter Fourteen

VALENTINE'S DAY DAWNED bright, sunny, and surprisingly warm for a February day in Idaho. I worked at both the newspaper and at Sam's with one eye on the clock, relieved when the work day was over.

Cade picked me up early, and I had worn a new red dress I had picked up on clearance at an after Christmas sale at the local dress shop. Cade wore a nice black suit with a red hanky in his pocket. He looked pretty spiffy and I couldn't help but admire him.

We had driven to the restaurant in Boise and the place was packed with couples celebrating the day of love. Cade pulled my chair out for me and I sat down. Each table was lit with candles while the overhead lights were dimmed. He had brought me a large bouquet of red and white roses that he had bought from my mother's shop.

"Your mother's flower shop was busy when I picked up your flowers," he said unfolding his napkin. "That's good news."

"That is good news. I wanted to wait until the end of the day before asking her how things were going. That way if things were a little slower early on, she wouldn't be discouraged. I always get more discouraged about something that isn't going well if I talk about it," I said.

He nodded. "I know what you mean," he said looking over the menu in front of him. "I hope things turn around for her. I think she holds a lot back."

"You can say that again. She can be smart-alecky when she wants to be, but as far as how things are going in her life, you rarely hear a peep out of her."

"Your Mom's funny. I really like her," he said looking at me and smiling.

"I know she is, and I know you do," I said and grinned. "What are you going to order?"

"I'm looking at the beef bourguignon," he said looking at the menu again.

"That sounds good. I think I'm going to get the lamb stew. Navarin," I said. "And for dessert, I'm definitely considering the Tarte Tatin."

"Oh," he said turning the menu over where the desserts were. "I didn't even see that. I might get the Paris-Brest and we can sample each other's dessert."

"I like the way you think," I said.

The waiter came and took our dinner and dessert orders and Cade ordered a bottle of red wine. I wasn't much of a drinker and neither was he, but it was Valentine's Day, so why not?

"So, Cade," I said, "What's going on with the case?" I had held back on the drive over and hadn't asked him anything about it. I knew he would rather focus on our date, but I had to know.

He narrowed his eyes at me. "You never quit, do you?"

I shook my head. "Of course not. And that's what you love about me. Now, what's going on?"

"I might have my eye on someone," he said. "But I really don't want to say who it is. I like having the element of surprise."

"Element of surprise? Do you think I'd run around town telling everyone who you thought the killer was?"

"Of course not," he said and chuckled. "Don't be so sensitive. I can't tell you everything and you know that."

I gave him the evil eye. "Sure. Keep your secrets."

He shrugged and tried to look cute. Which I might add, he achieved successfully.

"Adele seems to think Kate's the best candidate," I told him. "She said Kate filed a sexual harassment complaint against Arnold at work."

The look on Cade's face was priceless. "Somehow I just can't imagine that. I mean, Arnold sexually harassing anyone, not that she had filed a complaint."

"Neither can I. So what are you going to do?" The waiter arrived with the wine and offered to pour it for us. Cade gave him the go-ahead and when he had poured it and left, I turned back to Cade. "Well?"

"I'm going to continue investigating. Now then, let's stop talking about the case and let's talk about you."

I looked at him with surprise. "Talk about me? Why on earth would we talk about me?"

He chuckled. "Why wouldn't we talk about you? I talk about you all the time and I bet you don't even know it."

I narrowed my eyes at him. "Who are you talking about me to?"

He grinned and shrugged. "Wouldn't you like to know? I just have to say that I think this might be the happiest I've been in a really long time. And you know that's saying a lot."

I stared at Cade, speechless. When I asked Cade about his past or previous girlfriends, it wasn't that he avoided the questions, but he was just very perfunctory. He gave me the overall details, but nothing specific. I had the feeling that he had been on his own for a while before he moved to Sparrow.

"Well, I talk about you a lot too," I said. "What are you saying about me?"

He grinned devilishly. "Like I'm going to tell you."

I took a sip of my red wine and grimaced. There was a reason I didn't drink very often, and that reason was that I really didn't care for the taste of it. But occasionally, I gave it another try. It might not have been the best idea seeing as how I still didn't like it much.

"This isn't too bad, is it?" he asked, having just taken his own sip of wine.

"I was thinking it was kind of awful," I admitted.

He laughed. "You're such a romantic."

"You Know it."

I looked around the room at the tables of happy couples and smiled. Valentine's Day was the happiest day of the year when it came to newer relationships. My ex-husband had never been sentimental and once we were married, he had never remembered Valentine's Day. The first couple of years of our marriage, I had bought him gifts and dressed up on Valentine's Day, hoping he had made reservations somewhere for dinner. Each time I was disappointed when he looked at me like I was nuts. I hoped Cade would not follow suit. The roses had been sweet, and even though he had said he was going to get me flowers, I hadn't expected much. Even when my ex-husband and I had been dating, he hadn't done much for me where flowers were concerned, or any other gift. In retrospect, I wondered why I had ever stayed with him beyond the first couple of months.

The waiter returned with our food and my stomach growled. It smelled wonderful and I could hardly wait to dig in.

Cade cut into his beef bourguignon and took a bite, and grinned, nodding his head. "This is really good," he said when he'd swallowed.

I took a taste of my own lamb stew and groaned. "They make really great food here. I wonder if the chef has ever considered writing a cookbook?"

He chuckled. "How are you doing on that cookbook you're writing? Weren't you supposed to have it finished at the beginning of this year?"

I shrugged. "I guess I got a little behind on it, but it shouldn't be too much longer. I've already written a query letter and a synopsis to send out to agents. I'm getting excited about the possibility of working with another publisher."

"So even though you and your ex-husband have made up, there's no chance his publishing company would publish the book?"

I shook my head. "I wouldn't want them to. Honestly, after what I went through last year, I have no desire to be connected with him or his publishing company ever again. I feel like I'd be a fool if I fell for that again."

"I guess I can see your point," he said. "Hopefully you'll find an agent quickly."

"I think I will. I have a few contacts left in the industry that haven't been tainted by my ex-husband's smear campaign," I said and took another bite of my stew.

I could hardly wait to taste the Tarte Tatin I had ordered for dessert. I also wanted to taste Cade's Paris-Brest. As we talked and ate, my eyes landed on a small box in the middle of the table. Had it been there when we first got here? No, I was sure it hadn't been. And then it hit me that it was the size of a jewelry box. I looked up at Cade, eyes wide.

He smiled, and we stared he each other in silence for what felt like an incredibly long period of time. His eyes went to the box and then back to me.

"I just—got you a little something," he said haltingly.

I looked at the box again and felt my stomach heave. I wasn't ready for anything permanent. I was enjoying the relationship that Cade and I had together. Why did he have to go and ruin it?

I licked my lips, trying to figure out what to do now. I didn't want to hurt him, but I didn't want anything like what might be in that box.

"It's okay," he said and chuckled flatly. "It won't bite you."

"It might." I suddenly felt hot and faint and I wanted to go home. "I think we should go."

He stared at me. "Why? It's just—."

"It's just more than I bargained for," I cut him off.

"Rainey, will you just look at it?"

I shook my head and pushed my chair back. "I think I need to go home."

"Rainey, wait," he said and put his hand on my hand that was on the table as I was pushing my chair back. "It's not what you think it is. All it is—is a promise ring. A promise that I'll be here for you. Nothing more, nothing less."

I stared into his eyes as they desperately begged me not to leave. "What do you mean?"

"Just what I said. It's just a promise. I wanted to buy you something for Valentine's Day. That's all. I'll be here for you when you need me. And even if you don't need me, I'll be here."

I stared at him and then my eyes went to the box again. He nudged it toward me with his other hand. My free hand was shaking as I reach for the box and he released the hand he held. I opened it. It was a white gold ring with a thin band and a tiny chip of a diamond set in it. It was lovely and sweet and so much more than I knew what to do with.

"Thank you," I said because I couldn't think of anything else to say. It was sweet of him, but it still made me feel a little queasy.

"Don't freak out on me, Rainey," he said. "Let's finish our dinner. We've still got those wonderful desserts coming as soon as we're finished with our meals and I don't want to miss out on them. If you don't want the ring, I'll take it back. But think about it before you give it back to me."

I nodded. It was the least I could do. I took a sip of water and glanced at the ring in its box, still sitting on the table.

"It's a good thing I didn't plan on saying the L-word," he said without looking at me.

I swallowed and licked my dry lips again. "It's a good thing you didn't."

I picked up my spoon with a shaking hand and took another bite of my lamb stew. It would keep me from having to say anything else.

Chapter Fifteen

THE NEXT MORNING I stopped by Agatha's and picked up two large coffees to go. I had a double shot of espresso added to my latte to try to wake myself up. I think I was still in shock about what had happened the previous evening. I was crazy about Cade, don't get me wrong, but a ring was the last thing I had expected from him. Before I walked into the coffee shop, I slipped the ring into the front pocket of my jeans. I didn't want to have to explain it to Agatha, and I wasn't sure what kind of explanation I would give her, anyway. Cade had promised to be there for me. What more could I have asked for? Absolutely nothing. But I wasn't ready for anything permanent. I was glad he wasn't pushing, but I still wasn't sure how I felt about the ring.

After I picked up the coffees, I headed over to Mom's flower shop. I needed to know how Valentine's Day went. I hoped business had been booming, but I had a sinking feeling that it may not have been, in spite of what Cade had said about there being a lot of customers in the shop when he picked up my flowers. Cade didn't understand exactly how busy a flower shop could get on Valentine's Day and what he saw might have been mild compared to previous years.

Besides that, Gina's flower shop was still relatively new and it wouldn't have surprised me if people wanted to see what she was offering for Valentine's Day. I love living in a small town, but it had its drawbacks. There were only so many people to sell flowers to whether it was Valentine's Day or not. And even when there had been a competing flower shop in town in the past, she had always done well. People tended to be loyal in Sparrow, but it seemed that might not be the case anymore.

"Good morning, Mom," I said as I walked through the door. "Good morning Donna." I mentally kicked myself for not picking up a coffee for Mom's assistant, but then she picked up a coffee from behind the counter.

"Good morning, Rainey," Donna said, as she added a yellow bow to a daisy and carnation arrangement. "How are you this morning?"

"I'm doing well, thank you," I said and walked over to where Mom was standing at the other end the counter. "Look what I brought you."

"That's so sweet of you, Rainey," Mom said and took the coffee from me. "I can use it. I'm exhausted."

"Does that mean you had a very busy Valentine's Day?" I asked her.

She shrugged. "I guess you could say it was busy. But I'm not sure I would call it very busy."

"But it was better than what you thought it would be?" I asked, hopefully.

"A little," she said and shrugged. "How about you? How was your date with Cade?"

With the question, I could suddenly feel the weight of the ring in my front pocket. I wasn't going to bring that up just yet.

"It was nice," I said and took a sip of my coffee. "We went to that nice French restaurant in Boise and the food was absolutely delicious."

"Oh? What did you have for dessert?" she asked.

"Tarte Tatin," I told her. "It was wonderful."

"Oh my gosh," Donna exclaimed from the other end of the counter. "I've always wanted to go there. I told my husband that he better take me there one day. I told him I wanted to go for Valentine's Day, but he complained that it would be too busy, and he would take me another day."

"It was really busy," I agreed. "Cade made the reservation several weeks ago, I think."

"You better be nice to that man," Mom informed me. "He's the best thing you've ever seen."

"Thanks, Mom," I said sarcastically. She was right, of course. I had never dated anyone as wonderful as Cade.

"I'm just telling you the truth," she said and took another sip of her coffee. "This is really tasty. Thanks for picking it up for me."

"No problem," I said. "I'm really glad you had a better Valentine's Day than you thought you would have."

"Yeah, but it was down quite a bit from last year. That was even with Celia's flower shop open at the time." She shook her head. "I hate to jinx myself, but I'm afraid the slow business might last longer than I had anticipated."

I hated to hear her talk that way, but I was glad she was opening up about it. "Well then, we'll just have to come up with a plan to improve things around here."

"Well as soon as you come up with a plan, you let me know," she said and closed the order book she had in front of her.

"Hey Rainey," Donna said. "Is Cade any closer to catching Arnold Singer's killer?"

"He's working on it," I said. I couldn't go into any details and I was sure she understood that.

She nodded. "Isn't poor Adele going to be in a fix now?"

"Yes, I can't imagine how hard it is, losing your husband like that," I said, leaning on the counter.

She nodded. "There's that, and then there's the loss of that money from his post office job. He was there a long time, so I'm sure he got paid well," she said. "You know how Adele is, she loves to shop."

I glanced at her sideways. "I guess I don't know that about her," I said, turning to face her now. Even though we had seen the menagerie of gnomes and wooden people out front and then the frogs, fairies, and mushrooms on the inside of the house, I wasn't sure if that was what she was referring to, or if there was something else.

"Oh yeah," she said. "She and I go way back. She's always enjoyed shopping. Every time I see her, she shows me something new that she bought. And now she doesn't have Arnold's income to spend." She chuckled. "Of course, if she had life insurance on him, I suppose she doesn't need the income."

I was a little taken aback by the way Donna was speaking about Adele, but I was curious if she knew anything else. "I would imagine a lot of married couples have life insurance in case one of them dies."

She nodded. "I'm sure they do. Don't mind me, Rainey," she said. "I'm probably not being very kind. I've just always been surprised that she spends as much money as she does. Maybe I'm jealous. My husband would never let me spend money like that."

I glanced at Mom, who was watching Donna. "Adele was at work at the library when Arnold died," I pointed out.

Before Donna could answer me, the door swung open and Julie Rogers walked through the door. I smiled at her. She was Adele's coworker at the library.

"Good morning, Julie," Mom said to her. "How are you this morning?"

She smiled. "I'm fine. I was wondering if you had any leftover Valentine's Day arrangements that you're selling for cheap?" She blushed and continued. "I guess I shouldn't say it like that, should I? But my husband is the cheapest man in the world, and he gave me ten dollars to come and buy my own flowers this morning." She shrugged.

"Of course we do," Mom said. "You pick out whatever you want that says happy Valentine's Day in the display case there and I'll let you have it for ten dollars."

"Really? Anything?" she asked, brightening.

"Anything," Mom said.

Julie peered into the refrigerated display case. It didn't take her long before she pulled out the largest vase of red roses and pink daisies in the shop. There were little plastic cupids stuck in it and a ribbon that said happy Valentine's Day tied around it. Mom could have removed the ribbon and cupids and sold it for full price, but it was sweet she was letting Julie have it for ten dollars.

"I love this," she said and brought it up to the front counter and set it down. "That's so sweet of you, Mary Ann."

"Only for you, Julie," she said and went around to the other side of the counter to ring up her purchase.

"Julie," I said. "How is Adele doing? I know this has got to be so terribly hard for her, losing Arnold like she has."

She looked at me and frowned. "I guess she's doing as well as can be expected. It's a terrible shame."

I nodded. "It certainly is," I agreed. "It must have been such a shock when the police came to the library to tell her what happened."

She stared at me for a moment. Then she nodded. "It really was. You never expect to receive that kind of news."

"What kind of shift do you and Adele worked there at the library during the weekdays?" Mom asked.

Julie turned to her and hesitated, looking away. She looked back at Mom and smiled at her. "Well, that day both Adele and I opened the library, and we worked until 3:30. Or rather, we both would have worked until 3:30, but Adele went home early for obvious reasons."

"What time is opening time?" Mom asked.

Julie pasted an uneasy smile on her face. "We usually get there around 8:30. Sometimes earlier. We like to catch up or maybe put books out on the shelf if we didn't get everything put back the night before."

"Poor Adele," Mom said, as she rang up the flowers. "That'll be ten dollars. No tax for you."

Julie handed her the money and grinned at her. "You just made my day! Thanks again," Julie said and headed for the door with her arrangement.

When the door closed behind her, Mom turned to me. "She didn't sound very sure about Adele opening the library, did she?"

"I don't know, maybe. Maybe not." I wasn't sure if Julie was uncomfortable talking about Adele and her husband's murder, or if there were something she wasn't telling us. But if Adele was at the library as she said, there was no way Adele could have killed Arnold. If she wasn't telling the truth, I couldn't imagine why she would lie about it.

SAM HAD PUT THE IDEA in my head to make Boston cream cupcakes. I loved the idea, so I had been working on a recipe. I loved anything with a cream filling, so this was right up my alley. I wanted the cream to be more of a pudding consistency than light and airy, and I had to be careful that I didn't make the pudding too heavy and dense for the delicate cake.

I so far had tried three different versions of the recipe and I thought this last one was going to be a winner. I made a batch of them and decided to drop off six of them to Margaret Singer on my way to work at the newspaper. I would bring the rest of them to work with me so my coworkers could try them out. If they were a hit with everyone at the newspaper, I'd make another batch and bring them in for Sam to try.

I knocked on Margaret's door and waited for her to answer. She had been on my mind the last few days and I wanted to check on her to see how she was faring after the funeral. I knew this had to be hard on her, losing her only child, and I wondered if she had other relatives here in Sparrow. Being alone at her advanced age would be crushing.

Margaret opened the door and looked at me wide-eyed. "Rainey! I was just thinking about you and your sister and mother. What brings you to this side of town?"

I smiled and held the plate of cupcakes out to her. "I was trying out a new recipe for Boston cream cupcakes and I thought I'd bring some by for you. How are you doing, Margaret?"

The smile left her face as she looked at me somberly. "It's been hard," she said, nodding. "Would you like to come in?"

"Sure, I've got a few minutes before I have to be at my job at the newspaper."

I followed her into the living room and took a seat on the sofa, setting the plate of cupcakes on the coffee table. I appreciated Margaret's living room, comfy and cozy and done in neutral colors. A stark contrast to her daughter-in-law's living room.

"That's so sweet of you to think of me," she said. "How are your mother and sister?"

"Oh they're fine," I said. "We were just talking about you yesterday and wondering how you were doing. I told them I would stop in and say hello."

She nodded. "I don't think it's sunk in yet. I don't know how long something like that takes to happen, but it just doesn't feel real to me that my only boy is gone." She clasped her hands together in her lap and sighed.

"I just can't imagine," I said. I wondered about what Alice had said about Margaret being a member of the gun club. I just couldn't picture it.

"Does the detective have any idea who might have done it yet?" she asked.

"He doesn't tell me everything he knows," I said. "But I know he's hoping to make an arrest soon." It wasn't a lie. Cade had mentioned that he was hoping to make an arrest, and I hoped he was as close as he thought he was.

"I certainly hope so," she said. "I tell you, Rainey, maybe I shouldn't say it, but I still think it was Alice Garber. She's such a bitter old thing. She warned Arnold that if he didn't give her the money back for that refrigerator, he was going to be sorry."

I nodded. "I know Cade has been looking into this." I didn't want to say much more than that. I knew Cade had interviewed Alice when I was with him and he had let it slip when we had gone out on Valentine's Day that he had talked to her again. I hoped she hadn't completely lost her mind and killed Arnold without understanding what she had done. I didn't want to mess things up by saying something I shouldn't if he decided differently.

"She's become so strange these days," she continued. "Honestly, I wouldn't be surprised if it was her. She has a gun, you know."

"I do know about that," I said. "She said she bought it when her home was broken into a few years ago. She also said she was a member of the gun club and that you were a member." I didn't know how else to say it and I hope she didn't get offended by it.

"Yes, I am a member of the gun club. There's a senior citizen's chapter, you know," she said.

"Really? I had no idea," I said. I wondered how many of Sparrow's senior citizens were packing heat.

"Yes, Susan Martin started the chapter several years ago when we had a rash of break-ins around town. She thought it would be a good idea if we older folk armed ourselves and learned how to shoot. She found somebody that gave us lessons at a discount, you know."

"No, I didn't know that. That's not a bad idea, I suppose," I said. "In this day and age, it's always good to know how to defend yourself." I wasn't big on guns, but when you lived in Idaho where there was a lot of hunting and fishing, gun ownership was common among local citizens.

She nodded. "Yes, sometimes people think that because you're older, they can take advantage of you. But I'll tell you something, if somebody decides they're going to break into my home, they're going to get a really big surprise. It turns out I'm a pretty good shot and I'm not afraid to use my gun."

"Well, good for you in wanting to defend yourself," I said. "What kind of gun do you have?"

"Oh it's a 9mm," she said.

"Really? 9mm?" I wondered if Cade knew about Margaret's gun.

She nodded. "It's not a terribly large gun, and that's what I wanted. I wanted something that would shoot a large enough bullet that if I ever had to use it on someone, they'd know they'd been shot." She chuckled. "Just call me a pistol-packing granny." Then she sobered. "Except I'm not a granny at all, am I?"

It made me sad that Margaret had wanted grandchildren so badly and never got them. "I'm sorry you didn't get to have grandchildren of your own," I said. "But don't you still volunteer at the local elementary school helping the kids read?"

She brightened. "Yes I do," she said, nodding. "It's only one day a week, but it's the highlight of my week. Those little ones are so much fun to read with."

The idea that Margaret Singer helped the elementary school kids learn to read along with that head full of graying hair strengthened my conviction that she couldn't have killed her son. I had been wrong before of course, but I didn't think I was this time. 9mm gun or no, if she could have found it in her heart to kill her only child, then she was one of the best actresses around.

"I'm sure many of those children think of you as their grandmother in some way," I told her.

She settled back into the loveseat she was sitting on. "I have had one or two of them slip and call me grandma from time to time. They catch themselves, but it always makes me feel good."

I glanced at the clock on the wall. I needed to get going if I was going to be at work on time. "Well, Margaret," I said. "Don't hesitate to pay me or my mother and sister a visit whenever you feel lonely. My sister has plenty of kids and they would be thrilled to have another grandmother figure in their lives, and I know Stormy would think it was a wonderful idea."

"Do you think so?" she asked thoughtfully.

"I know so," I said. "I better get to work now. I hope you enjoy the cupcakes and don't be a stranger."

I got to my feet, and she walked me to the door. "Thanks again for the cupcakes," Margaret said.

"You're welcome."

I headed to my car. Margaret Singer did own the same caliber of gun that killed her son, and she admitted that she was an excellent shot, but I didn't see how she could be so heartless as to kill her son.

Chapter Sixteen

"WELL," SAM SAID EYEING the cupcakes I was putting into the covered display case. "What do we have here?"

I turned and grinned at him. "I think these just might be Boston cream cupcakes."

His eyes got big. "Boston cream cupcakes? How on earth did you think of something like that?"

I shrugged. "I guess maybe somebody may have suggested them and I may have taken that suggestion and given it a try. I've never made them before, but I think they turned out pretty well if I do say so myself."

"I bet they did," he said, his eyes on the cupcakes again. "I don't suppose you're going to let your boss have one, are you?"

"I could be persuaded," I said and chuckled. "Would you like one, Sam?"

"You know I would," he said.

I held the plate out to him and he took one of the cupcakes. "I used a yellow cake recipe for the cupcakes and put some wonderful pudding in the middle and topped it with chocolate icing." I thought I had done a pretty good job of duplicating the flavor of an actual Boston cream pie.

"Looks wonderful," he said and took a bite of it. He groaned and nodded. After he had swallowed, he said, "these are perfect. I don't think I'm going to be able to stop myself at just one."

"You help yourself to as many as you'd like, Sam," I said and closed the display case. You're the best boss I've ever had, and as such, you are entitled to as many cupcakes as you want."

"Aw, you're so sweet, Rainey." He took another cupcake, gave me the thumbs up, and headed back into the kitchen. We had had a snowstorm overnight and the snow plows hadn't yet hit the street the diner was on, so we didn't have any customers yet. We'd been promised that the snow plows would be by soon, and so we were waiting. It was times like this that I knew Sam wished he had just kept the diner closed for the day. The cupcakes would help brighten his day.

I watched as some poor soul out on the sidewalk struggled against the wind and snow. The wind had calmed down a little from what we had seen in the middle of the night, but it was still fairly brisk. I sighed and wished for my warm bed.

When I realize that poor soul outside was heading for the diner door, I hurried over and opened it, and realized it was Kate Janz with the mail. She pushed her way through the door and I closed it behind her to keep the wind out.

"Oh my gosh, Rainey," Kate breathe hard. "Can you believe the weather out there?"

"It's something else, isn't it? You should've just hung onto the mail and brought it by tomorrow when the weather might be better. I'm sure there isn't anything in it that we have to have today," I told her and helped her brush snow off her jacket.

She chuckled. "Now Rainey," she said. "You know the mail carrier motto; neither snow, nor rain, nor heat, nor gloom of night stays these couriers from the swift completion of their appointed rounds." She laughed again, and I wondered if she quoted that motto every chance she got.

I smiled. "Well, I guess if the post office is determined to get the mail delivered no matter what, they found the right person to do it."

"You better believe it," she said proudly. "No one out-delivers Kate Janz. My job is just too important to be lazy about it. I can't imagine being like some of the other post office employees. They have the attitude that they'll deliver mail when they get around to it. But people depend on me! I can't let them down."

I finished helping her brush the snow off her coat and I had to smile again. "It's good to see someone that takes their job so seriously." I thought she was going overboard with it, but if it made her happy, then who was I to say any different?

She nodded and walked up to the front counter, spying the display plate of cupcakes. "I can't let people down. It's just not in my nature to slack off. I don't want to speak ill of the dead, but Arnold Singer was not cut of the same cloth that I am. If people got their mail on time, then they got their mail on time. And if they didn't get it on time, they didn't get it on time. Some people just have that kind of attitude and Arnold was one of those people."

I frowned. The comment grated on my nerves. We had never received mail late in all the years that Arnold had delivered it, and I didn't appreciate her saying awful things about him now that he was gone and couldn't defend himself.

"I'm sure Arnold did the best he could," I said, biting back the words I really wanted to say.

She nodded but didn't take her eyes off the cupcakes. "Those look really delicious," she said. "What kind are they?"

"Those are Boston cream cupcakes," I said. "They're only a dollar."

She looked disappointed. "Really? A dollar? Arnold said he always got free baked goods when he came in here."

I sighed. I'd heard this before. "I'm surprised he said that because it really isn't true," I said firmly. She was hinting for that cupcake, and I suppose I could have been nice and given it to her, but after the comment she had made about Arnold, I wasn't in the mood to be nice.

"Oh," she said. "Maybe I misunderstood what he meant. They sure do look good."

"They are good," I said. "You better buy one while they're still here, because as soon as the snow plows come through and the customers start coming in, I'm sure they'll go fast."

She bit her lower lip, eyeing the cupcakes. "Well, I guess a dollar isn't too much to pay."

I rolled my eyes. If I were charging full price for them, I'd charge at least three dollars, but I didn't say as much. I opened the display case and removed one for her and placed it on some napkins on the front counter. Then I headed over to the cash register.

"That will be a dollar," I said. I wasn't going to charge tax, although I had half a mind to do it just because of what she said about Arnold.

She followed me over to the cash register and began digging in her pockets for a dollar. "Say, Rainey," she said as she dug. "Has Cade figured out who killed Arnold?"

I shook my head. "He hasn't made an arrest yet, but he said he was close to it. I'd sure hate to be in that person's shoes. Prison can't be much fun."

Her eyes went wide. "You'd think people would think about that sort of thing before they commit a crime, wouldn't you?"

I nodded. "You would think so. I'd hate to be facing prison. You know Kate, I heard a funny thing the other day."

She looked at me as she pulled a crumpled dollar bill from her pocket and handed it to me. "You did? What did you hear?"

"That you claimed Arnold sexually harassed you at work. I just can't imagine Arnold doing something like that." I straightened out the dollar bill and put it into the cash register without taking my eyes off of her. Sam would reimburse me later for the cupcakes we sold.

"What? How did you hear that? I mean, that's not something that should be known to just anyone," she said as her face went pale.

I shrugged. "You know how it is. Sparrow is a small town and things get around. Like I said, I just can't imagine Arnold doing something like that." I looked at her questioningly and waited.

She shook her head slowly. "I think it was just a misunderstanding. That's all. A misunderstanding."

"That's what I thought," I said, nodding. "Just a misunderstanding. Still, it takes a lot of gall to say something like that about someone when it's not true. So tell me Kate, why did you say it?"

She gritted her teeth together and took the stack of mail she had in her hand and slammed it down on the hostess station. "You know what, Rainey? It isn't any of your business. I had nothing to do with Arnold's murder, if that's what you're getting at. It was his wife, Adele. I'm telling you right now, she killed him because she couldn't stand him. She had a thing for spending money, and he didn't like it. But she wasn't going to let him stand in her way."

"How do you know?" I asked suspiciously. Donna had said the same thing, but I hadn't thought much of it at the time.

"Because I'm a mail carrier. I deliver mail and I filled in for Arnold when he couldn't make the rounds. I would take dozens of catalogs at a time to their house and to the library. She's always ordering things. Packages come into the post office all the time for her. Arnold was so embarrassed about it. You should've seen his face one day when she had thirty-two boxes come into the post office in one day. Thirty-two! Everybody teased him and kidded him about it, but he didn't like it. He turned bright red when everyone kept talking about it."

I couldn't imagine why this had anything to do with Arnold's death. "So? So she likes to go shopping. What does that mean?"

"She killed him because they couldn't afford to spend the money and he was always buying things for his mother. She resented him for spending the money on his mother when she wanted to spend it on herself. Now, I'm going to take my cupcake and I'm going to leave. And I'll advise you to keep your nose out of my business. And if I hear that you've been spreading rumors about me, saying I made a complaint about Arnold sexually harassing me, I'll bring a lawsuit against you. Defamation of character." She spun around, went back to the counter, picked up the cupcake, and stormed out of the diner.

I watched her go, thinking about what she had said. I was still convinced she had killed Arnold, but there was something about what she said about Adele's shopping habits that bothered me. If Adele collected life insurance on her husband, maybe she was going to go on a great big shopping binge.

But there was something bizarre about Kate, and if she would go to the extent of lying about something as serious as sexual harassment, something that might have cost Arnold his job, then I thought it was possible she might resort to murder to be rid of him.

Chapter Seventeen

AFTER SOME THOUGHT, I decided that Kate Janz was still my top pick as Arnold Singer's killer. I didn't care who she pointed her finger at; she was the one who had the most reason to do it. She had embarrassed herself by claiming Arnold had sexually harassed her at work and she would have needed a way to vindicate herself. I didn't know why she would accuse him, to begin with, although it made me wonder if she might have had an interest in him and he had rejected her. That was my best guess at the moment.

Alice Garber was my second pick. But I didn't think she would have done it on purpose, even though Margaret claimed she had reason to do it. Alice was angry about the refrigerator, but no one in their right mind would kill someone over that. I thought her mind might be slipping just enough that she had gotten frightened at some sound in the neighborhood and had shot at a shadow, hitting Arnold accidentally. She might be too afraid to admit what she had done. I hoped that was how it happened because, in her current mental state, a judge would be more apt to be lenient with her. We could chalk it up as just a terrible accident, and maybe Alice would go to some facility that could help her in her final years.

The snow and wind had finally stopped, and the plows had come through town and cleared out the streets. By the time I was finished with my shift at the diner, the sun was shining, and the streets were clear. I found myself driving by the county library. The parking lot had already been cleared and so I pulled in and parked. I didn't believe what Kate said about Adele, but it had sparked my curiosity. I couldn't imagine anybody getting dozens of catalogs at a time, let alone dozens of packages delivered to their door in one day. Both she and Arnold worked at jobs where they had been employed for many years and probably made pretty decent money at this point in their lives, but I still couldn't imagine someone spending the money that both Kate and Donna said Adele spent. Sure, I had seen the inside of Adele's home, and she did like to collect things, but that didn't mean anything.

I pushed open the library door and was taken back to my childhood when my mother would bring my sister and me here during the summer and we would join the summer reading program. Each year there was a different theme and we would hurry to read enough books to win a prize at the end of the summer. One year the prize at the end of the summer was a barbecue put on by the library staff. The first book read earned the plate, and subsequent books read earned a different paper cut-out food item that we colored in and attached to the plate. At the end of the summer, we turned in our paper plates with glued on food for the real thing. Mine and Stormy's plates were stuffed with paper food and we had a feast at the barbecue.

There was a display of newly acquired children's books and I looked them over. Stormy's youngest girls would love to read some of these books. I picked up a picture book about a mouse that was resisting her bedtime and flipped through it. Why hadn't I brought the girls down here to check out books? I was going to put it on my list of things to do, including bringing them for the reading program this summer. My nephew Curtis was a bookworm, and I was sure he made good use of the library, but I hadn't brought him since he was five or six and I felt like I was falling behind in my auntie duties for not having brought my nieces here.

"Hi Julie," I said when she came around the corner with an armload of books.

She stopped and smiled. "Hi Rainey," she said. "How are you doing today?"

"Well this morning I wasn't feeling so great about getting out into the weather, but now I'm great," I said. "I just got off work, the streets have been plowed, and the sun's out. I couldn't be doing any better if I tried."

She laughed. "I hear you," she said. "I was feeling exactly the same way this morning when that wind was blowing. I can't wait for summer, it feels like it's been winter for eons."

"I know what you're saying," I agreed. "Summer is always a long time in coming."

"We just got a bunch of new books in the other day," she said. "We got a donation from the private sector and it was a lot of fun picking out new books. What do you like to read?"

"Oh," I said thinking about it. The truth was I hadn't read a book in a while. "I like mysteries and historical novels."

"We've got new books in both of those genres," she said. "You should come and take a look at all the new books we got in."

"I think I will," I said, and I followed her over to a rack of books that she was putting out onto the shelves.

"Oh, this one looks good," I said picking up a cozy mystery with a picture of books and a cat on the front.

"I love that series," she said, nodding. "I love books in just about every genre though."

"Then I guess you have the right job, don't you?" I said looking around the library. "Is Adele around?"

She shook her head. "No, she had some business to attend to this morning, but she'll be in later in the afternoon. Is there something I can help you with?"

"Oh, no, I was just going to say hello to her and ask how she was doing. She's been on my mind a lot since Arnold died."

She nodded and made a clucking sound. "I just couldn't believe it when I heard it," she said. "I hope the police are able to find the killer soon. He was a nice guy and I don't know who would want to kill him."

"I know they've been working hard on the case. Arnold was such a nice guy, and to think that somebody could have just gone up to him and shot him in the middle of the day like that is beyond anything I could imagine. I mean, I would think it would have to be somebody that he knew, or else he wouldn't have allowed them to approach his mail truck like that." I waited.

She looked at me. "I don't know about that," she said slowly. "I mean, Arnold was a trusting guy. Maybe a stranger walked up to him and asked him for directions, and he didn't see the gun until it was too late."

I nodded. "I suppose that's a possibility," I said, hoping she would say more if there was something else to be said. "But that person would have to know his mail route unless there was a stranger that just wanted to randomly kill someone. But then, why would they choose a mailman to kill?"

She paused with the stack of books still in her hands and looked at me. "I know. I've racked my brain about how it might have happened. It doesn't make any sense to me because anyone that knew Arnold would know how harmless he was."

"Harmless is the right word for him," I said looking at her. And then I knew it. She knew something more than she was letting on.

She bit her lower lip and looked to the right and then to the left and then back at me. "Do you really think it was someone that knew him well?"

I nodded. "I really do. I think somebody had something against him for some reason and they decided to get rid of what they considered a problem. I don't think Arnold himself honestly would have provoked someone to murder, but sometimes people don't need a genuine reason to murder."

She nodded slowly and stared at me. "You know, there's something that's been on my mind for a while. And I probably shouldn't even say this, but it's been bothering me a little." She suddenly sounded anxious. "This one thought keeps coming back to me."

"What is that?"

"Well, it's probably nothing," she said and picked up another book from the rack with her free hand and looked at me again. "It's just that Adele went and got coffee that morning. When she came back to work, she seemed, I don't know. Nervous? No, maybe nervous isn't the word for it. But almost excited. She kept talking really fast. She had bought me a coffee and when she gave it to me, she just kept saying over and over that she had gotten me a coffee with an extra shot of espresso and she had gotten herself a double shot of espresso and she was feeling the effects of the caffeine." She stopped talking and looked at me.

"How long was she gone?"

"I really don't remember, but I do remember thinking she had been gone a long time to just be picking up coffee. Like maybe close to forty-five minutes," she said, looking away. Then she turned back to me. "I really don't think she could have hurt Arnold. Honestly. She isn't that kind of person."

I nodded. "Did you mention this to the police?"

She shook her head. "I didn't even think about it. I was so stunned when I heard the news that it didn't occur to me until later. You don't think there's a possibility—do you?"

I smiled. "Not really," I said. "But it's always good to give the police any information that you might think of." I didn't know what to make of what she had told me, but I didn't want to alarm her and make her think I thought there was a possibility Adele had killed her husband. I also didn't want her to mention to Adele that she had talked to me about it. I smiled. "Well, I think I'm just going to check out this book and get going."

We headed to the front desk so I could check out my book. I had a sinking feeling about Adele. Cade would need to check into it.

Chapter Eighteen

WHEN I GOT INTO MY car I had planned to go home and snuggle up in front of the fireplace with the mystery book I had checked out of the library. But something Julie said kept eating at me. The library was just a few blocks away from two coffee shops. One of them was Agatha's shop. If Adele had gone to pick up a couple of coffees, even if there had been a long line, it wouldn't have taken her anywhere close to forty-five minutes. It would take fifteen minutes. If there happened to be a really long line, maybe twenty minutes, including the time it took to drive back to the library. Even if she walked, she could have easily been at either coffee shop within minutes.

I pulled my phone out of my purse and gave Cade a call. When he answered on the third ring, I said, "how close are you to making an arrest in Arnold Singer's death?"

"Hey," he said, chuckling. "Hi Rainey. I'm doing fine, and I miss you so much. I'm so glad you called to check on me."

"Hi Cade," I said good-naturedly. "I miss you so much, how are you doing today?"

"I'm doing great," he said. "And regarding your first question, I really can't say. We have someone in our sites, but we need to get a search warrant for the gun."

I thought about this. "How long does it take to get a search warrant?"

"Not long. We expect to have it in the next day or so. Why?"

"Because I just talked to Julie Rogers at the county library. Adele Singer left to get coffee the day of Arnold's murder and she was gone about forty-five minutes. I can't imagine it would have taken more than twenty minutes, even if either of the coffee shops she went to was packed."

"I know there are a couple of coffee shops near the library, but there are also a couple of others around town. Maybe she went there?"

"Is Adele Singer the person you are getting a search warrant for?" I asked. She could have gone to another coffee shop, but why would she?

"Rainey, don't put me on the spot. Why aren't you at work? Don't you have something to do today?"

"I finished my shift at Sam's, and I don't have to go to the newspaper today."

There was a pause. "Rainey, promise me you will behave yourself and find something to do. I'm sure there are recipes to create for your cookbook. Which, by the way, you still haven't found a publisher for. Maybe that's a good use of your time this afternoon?"

I sighed. "Fine. I'll go home and I'll make something. If you're lucky, maybe I'll even make something for dinner."

"That's what I want to hear," he said. "I love you, Rainey. Behave yourself."

I snorted and hung up. You would've thought Cade would have known me better by now. And then I stopped. He said the L-word. I breathed out and shook myself. I'd worry about that later.

I drove over to Adele's house. I didn't expect her to be there, but I wanted to check out that gnome collection again. How much could those possibly cost? And those wooden people? I couldn't imagine they'd be terribly expensive, but I could be wrong. Maybe those things were collector's items and people might pay more for a certain manufacturer. I've seen crazier things before.

As I pulled up in front of Adele's house, I idled my car and looked the collection over. There were a lot of gnomes and wooden people, but no way could they be worth more than a few hundred dollars. A thousand, tops. If she had been collecting them over the past ten years or more, it wasn't much money at all. With the way Kate talked, you would think Adele had to be spending a lot more money than that. I was just about to pull away, having decided Kate was out of her mind, and that Adele had probably gone to one of the coffee shops across town for some reason the morning Arnold died, when Adele's car pulled into the driveway. I looked over at Adele and she was staring right at me. Busted. I smiled, and I shut my car off, got out, and tried to come up with a reason for being in front of her house.

"Hi Rainey," she called after getting out of her car.

"Hi Adele," I said, smiling at her. "How are you today?"

She gave me a sad smile. "Oh you know," she said. "I guess I'm doing as well as can be expected."

I walked over to where she stood in the driveway. "You've been on my mind lately, and I thought I'd just stop by and see how you were doing."

She nodded. "I sure do appreciate that. Would you like to come in?"

"Sure," I said and followed her into the house. I glanced around at all the items she had in the living room as she led me into the kitchen.

"Would you like some tea?" she asked, turning to look at me.

"I'd love some," I said and glanced around the kitchen. She had ceramic fruit all over the kitchen. There were a number of wall hangings, fruit-shaped spice jars, and fruit covered rugs on the floor. A set of canisters in the shape of apples lined her countertop. "My, you are a collector, aren't you?"

She chuckled as she got a box of tea out of the cupboard. "I am. My mother always said I was a little crazy, but when I like something, I like it and I've got to have it."

Kate's words came back to me and I wondered if she was right. "It's fun to collect things, isn't it? When I was a kid, I had to have every Beanie Baby I could get my hands on."

She laughed and turned to me again as she filled a teapot with water. "Me too! In fact, one of my spare bedrooms is devoted to Beanie Babies and dolls." She shook her head and grinned. "Arnold always said I was going overboard, but I didn't care. We didn't have any kids to spoil, so why not spoil myself?"

"I hear you," I said. "I don't have kids, either, and I tend to indulge myself from time to time." I looked around the room again. "Do you get Arnold's pension now that he's passed?"

She turned on the burner beneath the teakettle. "His pension? Yes, the post office provides a nice pension. Plus, Arnold had the foresight to take out life insurance on both of us. That will help me get through. I do okay at the library, but Arnold was the real breadwinner."

I stared at her, surprised she admitted to the life insurance and pension. Of course, she didn't know that I knew what I knew. "Without the pension and the life insurance, I would imagine it would be very difficult for you to continue collecting things, wouldn't it?"

She stopped smiling and turned back to the teakettle. "I suppose it would," she admitted. "We took out a second on the mortgage, and it would be really hard for me to make both payments if I didn't have more money than my salary coming in."

I stared a hole in Adele's back as she took two teacups out of the cupboard.

"It really bothered you that he was giving money to his mother, didn't it? Buying her things when you could have used the money to buy something for yourself?"

She spun around and stared at me. "What do you mean by that?"

"You thought that was your money and it should be spent on your collections. And when he wouldn't listen to you and kept spending money on his mother, it made you angry, didn't it?" I slowly reached my hand into my front jeans pocket where I had tucked my cell phone.

Her jaw tightened. "Rainey, I don't know what you're talking about. Sure, his mother is a pest and always whined and cried about needing this or that, but I never objected to him buying things for her. It was his mother after all, and even if she really didn't like him much, it was his prerogative to spend money on her."

I nodded. "Did you kill your husband, Adele?" I probably shouldn't have asked it, but we both knew the truth and there was no reason not to get it out there in the open. I slipped my phone out of my pocket.

"That's the craziest thing I've ever heard," she said and swallowed hard. "Rainey, I'm going to have to ask you to leave. I don't like those kinds of accusations. You know as well as I do that his mother killed him. If it wasn't her, then it was that nutty Alice Garber. That woman is crazy as a loon and everyone knows it."

"You got it. I'll leave." I nodded and turned to go. I heard one of the kitchen drawers open and close quickly and a cold chill went down my back.

"Wait, Rainey," she said calmly, and I turned around. She held a small gun in her hand. "I can't have you spreading rumors about me around town, Rainey."

I nodded. "I didn't think you could," I said. I made a mental note to find a gun small enough that would fit into a pocket if I was going to continue to confront possible murder suspects.

"Let's go get in my car," she said calmly. "Don't try anything funny or I'll shoot you dead right here in the kitchen."

I nodded and slowly turned toward the kitchen doorway. As we walked across the living room, my phone slipped out of my sweaty hand. When it hit the floor, I cried out, "oh!" Then I grabbed a ceramic mushroom from an end table and turned and hurled it at her face as hard as I could. I had been on the girls' softball team when I was a senior in high school, and I was just as surprised as Adele was that I could still pitch a fastball.

She screamed as the mushroom made contact with her face and the gun flew from her hand, clattering to the floor. I rushed over and grabbed it, then picked up my phone and dialed 911 while Adele cursed me and scrambled on the floor to get her bearings.

Chapter Nineteen

"FUNNY, I SEEM TO RECALL that the last thing I told you was to be good and stay out of trouble," Cade said.

I was leaning up against my car as an ambulance took Adele away. I really didn't think she needed an ambulance. She only asked for one to be dramatic and gain the police officers' sympathies. She cursed me as they wheeled her past me on a stretcher. Call me heartless, but I didn't feel the least bit sorry for her.

"Are you sure that was me you were talking to?" I asked him.

"Rainey, it isn't funny. You could have been killed," he said. "As it is, Adele is claiming you broke into her house with that gun and smashed her in the face with a ceramic mushroom. Why did you hit her in the face with a ceramic mushroom?"

"I didn't have the heart to smash a fairy," I said.

He closed his eyes and shook his head, trying to suppress a grin. "Seriously, Rainey," he said. "You've got to stop this kind of thing. I don't know how you're even alive at this point."

"It's because I have a mean fast pitch," I said. I may have sounded nonchalant and like this was something that I did all the time, but the truth was that I was pretty freaked out about what had happened. I couldn't even remember making the decision to pick up that mushroom and slam it at her face, but I was glad I had.

He leaned on my car, next to me. "Please don't do this anymore."

I nodded but didn't say anything. I had never intended to do some of the things I had done in recent months. They just happened the way they had, and I was thankful I was still alive.

"So she won't admit that she killed Arnold?" I finally asked.

"She did at first. Said she flagged him down while he was delivering the mail and did what she had to do. She shot him and let his mail truck roll down the road. Said she couldn't let him keep giving her money away to his mother."

I nodded without looking at him. "Sad."

"Then she suddenly changed her story and said you broke into her house and tried to rob her."

"I did have my eye on those purple fairies with the gossamer wings. They would have looked nice in my bathroom."

"I took you for more of a gnome woman. What is up with that house, anyway? It's bizarre," he said, glancing at it.

"The mind of a crazy woman knows no bounds," I explained.

"Speaking of crazy women, she said she thought you were unstable and had probably killed Arnold."

I laughed. "Wow. Just, wow."

He chuckled and we were silent again. Then he looked at my hands. "I seem to recall having given you a ring on Valentine's Day," he said after a minute or two of silence.

I clenched my fists together. Then I reached into my front pocket and pulled the ring out and slipped it on my right ring finger. "This one?"

He nodded and looked off into the distance. "You don't have to wear it if you don't want to."

"I want to," I said, and looked in the opposite direction.

"No, you don't want to. And it's fine. Really, I knew you probably weren't ready for it and I completely understand."

"It's not that I don't want to wear it," I said carefully. "It's that if I suddenly begin wearing it, everybody I know is going to start asking about it. And then I have to say no, it isn't an engagement ring, it's a promise ring. And then I have to go into why it's a promise ring. And I guess it's just easier to wear it in my pocket."

"It doesn't have to be a promise ring," he said without looking at me.

"What do you mean it doesn't have to be a promise ring?" I asked.

"It could be more than that," he said carefully.

We were treading on thin ice here. After a moment, I replied, "I like it being a promise ring. And if you don't mind, for a while, I think I'll just wear it in my pocket."

He chuckled lightly. "Why am I not surprised by that? Why would I ever be surprised by anything you do or say?"

"You really shouldn't be," I said. "You should just sit with bated breath, waiting to see what I'll say or do next."

"How do you know that isn't what I do already?"

I shrugged. "I just assumed you did."

He laughed again. "That is exactly what I do, believe it or not." He scooted over an inch, his arm touching mine. Then he leaned over and gave me a quick kiss. "Wear it wherever you like."

I nodded. "One of these days I'll be brave and wear it for the world to see. And then you can deal with my mother."

"I'll deal with your mother."

"Good. Because once she sees it, she'll be out of control. You'll never get a moment's rest."

"I guess I see where you get it from, then," he said.

"My father was much more laid back, and nice. Stormy takes after him."

We were quiet a few minutes again, and then he turned to me. "I L-word you."

I squeezed my eyes shut. "I might L-word, you too. But I can't swear to it just yet, and if you ever tell anybody that I L-word you, I'll tell them that you're lying. But, between the two of us, I probably do L-word you."

"I knew it," he said and chuckled. Without another word, he headed back inside Adele's house.

I watched him go and stuck one hand in my front jeans pocket and felt for the ring. Tears sprang to my eyes, and I blinked them back. I didn't know what I had done to deserve a complete do-over on my life, but I was grateful for it.

The End

Sneak Peek

Lemon Pie and a Murder
     A Rainey Daye Cozy Mystery, book 11
Chapter One

"What's going on over there?" I asked, joining Georgia Johnson where she stood near the front window at Sam's diner. We both had the early morning shift, and it was now just after 10:00 a.m. We were finally getting a break from the customers before the lunch shift began. Sam's diner was only open for breakfast and lunch, so we would get to go home soon, with Diane Smith and Luanne Merrill taking over the lunch shift.

Georgia glanced over her shoulder at me and narrowed her eyes. "How am I supposed to know? Do you think I read minds?" She snorted and walked away. I glanced over my shoulder at Diane. She had just arrived to prepare for the lunch crowd and was tying an apron around her waist.

"That one's a grump," she said and grinned. She joined me at the window. "I wonder what's going on over there? Someone opening a new business? We certainly could use more businesses around here."

We watched as several men walked in and out of the empty building across the street. It was spring in Sparrow, Idaho, and the warmer weather was making me happier by the day. While I enjoyed the winter, especially at Christmas time, I was ready for warm weather and sunshine.

"I don't know. That place has been empty for years now, but it looks like somebody's going to open up a business over there." That was good news. Sparrow was a tourist town with the Snake River recreation sites just outside of town. Any new business would help the town out and was a welcome sight.

We watched as two men walked into the shop, propping the door open behind them. "I hope it's a new bookstore," Diane said, turning to look at me. "We could use a good bookstore."

"A bookstore? I guess a bookstore would be nice, but we could use another clothing store. The few clothing stores we have are so outdated," I said. "And expensive."

"You can say that again," she agreed, glancing behind her as our boss, Sam Stevens, came out of the kitchen. He saw us at the window and came to look with us.

"What's going on over there?"

"We think someone's opening up a new business. Any ideas what it might be?" I asked. In a small town, news usually travels fast, but I hadn't heard a thing about a new business.

He shook his head slowly. "No, I haven't heard anything about it."

I nodded. "Well then, we're going to have to go over there and ask around, aren't we?" I needed to know what was going on over there.

"Yeah, I guess so," he said, still watching the building across the street. "You work at the newspaper. I thought you guys knew everything that goes on around here?"

I glanced at him. "I wouldn't say we know everything. But usually there's talk of this kind of thing, and I haven't heard a word. That's odd."

In a small town, any new business opening up is exciting. Sometimes you have to take your excitement where you can find it.

"I think I know that guy," Sam said, taking a step closer to the window and focusing on the two men that had just come back out of the building.

"Who is he?" I asked.

"Lucas Ford," Sam said slowly.

I turned to look at him. There was something in his voice when he said the name. He was frowning now.

"You don't sound excited about that," I pointed out.

He was quiet a minute, keeping his eye on the taller man. Then he shrugged and looked at me. "I don't care one way or another. A new business is good for the town, so I'm all for it."

"You can say that again," Diane agreed. "Sometimes I wish I lived in a bigger city. I hate having to drive over to Tahoe whenever I want to do any major shopping."

"I usually do a lot of my shopping online when I can't get what I need here in town," I said, turning away from the window. Currently, we only had one customer sitting in a corner booth. He was in Georgia's section, so I didn't have anything pressing to do. "I guess I could run the vacuum in here before the lunch hour rush." The floor wasn't messy, but I liked keeping the diner impeccably clean on my shifts.

"It's not that messy," Diane said, following behind me. "I think we're fine with just a little spot cleaning."

I nodded and went to get a white dishcloth from behind the front counter. It wasn't summer yet, but things had picked up around here on the weekends. We were enjoying a midweek breather from the increased business now, but come Friday, things would pick up again with the tourists that were taking a long weekend and enjoying the Snake River.

I glanced up as two white work trucks pulled up in front of the shop across the street. I glanced at Sam as he passed me on his way back into the kitchen. Curiosity may have killed the cat, but it was driving me nuts. "Sam, do you mind if I run across the street and see what's going on?"

He stopped, glancing at me. "Right now?"

I nodded and grinned. "You know how nosy I am. I've got to know the scoop. Besides, you want to know, too."

He chuckled and shook his head. "Make it fast in case we get busy while you're gone."

I waved a hand at him. "We aren't going to get busy. The morning rush is over and it's too early for lunch." I took my apron off and tucked it beneath the front counter, and looked at Diane. "Want to come with me?"

She nodded and removed her apron, stowing it beside mine. "Georgia, we'll be back in five minutes," she called over her shoulder.

"You both can't go!" Georgia put her hands on her hips and glared at us.

"Relax, we'll be back in five minutes," I said and headed through the front door before she had a chance to say anything else.

"She's going to be steamed when we get back," Diane said and chuckled.

"She's always steamed. May as well give her something to get steamed about."

She nodded. "Right?"

We hurried to the corner and across the four-lane street, and then casually sauntered up to the building. The workmen that had pulled up in the trucks were inside the building and the two men we had seen talking together stood just on the inside of the front door.

"Hello," I said brightly, walking up to the open door. "I'm going to take a wild guess and say that Sparrow is getting a new business."

The taller of the men looked at me and smiled. "You got that right. How are you ladies this morning?"

"We're doing great," I said, glancing around the empty building. "Don't keep us in suspense, what kind of business are you opening up?"

The taller of the two looked to be in his early thirties and had sandy blond hair. He stuck his hands in his trouser pockets and looked from me to Diane and back again. Then he grinned, flashing a million-dollar smile. "A diner."

My stomach dropped. "A diner?" I glanced over my shoulder at Sam's. "Right across the street from Sam's diner?"

He walked closer to us. "Sure. What better place than right across the street from that old greasy spoon? We'll give the fine folks of Sparrow a great place to eat. Of course, we'll put that hole in the wall dive out of business, but that's the way it goes." He laughed.

I felt my hackles rise, and I sensed Diane stiffening at the slight. "It's not a greasy spoon, it's the best food in Sparrow," she said.

The man chuckled. "I think you're being generous. Have you been in that place?"

My eyes went wide. "Of course we've been in there. We work there."

Now it was his turn to look surprised. "Oh, I had no idea. Well then, I guess we're going to be neighbors then." He looked both of us up and down. "And I'll be hiring waitresses, so you might want to put your applications in early. I'll pay you each a quarter more per hour than you're getting now and I'll give you someplace you can be proud to work."

I narrowed my eyes at him. "Sam's is one of the best places in town to work. I can't imagine working anywhere else and we're both proud to say we work there." I suddenly felt protective of Sam and the diner. I didn't know who this guy was, but I didn't like him.

He smiled easily, but he was the enemy and Diane and I both knew it. "Relax, we're going to offer something a little different than Sam's does. We're going for home-style cooking with a traditional menu like Mom used to make."

"What do you think Sam sells?" I asked. Diner food *was* home-style cooking.

He shook his head. "Sam sells traditional diner food. Greasy, overcooked, diner food."

Diane crossed her arms in front of herself. "You don't know what you're talking about. Sam's is the best food in town and there's nothing greasy about it."

He shrugged. "I guess if you've never had anything better, then you wouldn't know any better."

There was a smirk on the guy's face and I wanted to slap it right off of him.

"I think we're going to head back to work," I said. "I've heard all I need to hear."

He nodded. "You tell Sam that Lucas Ford said hello for me, will you?" He chuckled and glanced at his friend, and they both laughed.

"I sure will, and I'm sorry that you chose this location for a diner. Sam's Diner has an impeccable reputation and our customers are loyal." I turned around and headed back out the door with Diane hot on my heels.

When we had gotten away from the open door, Diane looked at me. "What do you think about that?" she hissed. "What a jerk."

"I think it takes a lot of nerve choosing to open a diner right across the street from Sam's. There are plenty of empty buildings around here that he could have moved into."

I knew it wasn't a coincidence that brought him to that building across the street from the diner. Whoever this Lucas Ford was, he was intentionally trying to infringe on Sam's business.

We hurried across the street and into the diner and headed for the kitchen where Sam stood in front of the grill.

"Sam!"

He turned to look at me. "What?"

"That Lucas Ford is opening a diner right across the street."

He was quiet a moment, then he turned back to the grill. "I was afraid of that."

Buy Lemon Pie and a Murder on Amazon

https://www.amazon.com/gp/product/B084YSWWRH

If you'd like updates on the newest books I'm writing, follow me on Amazon and Facebook:

https://www.facebook.com/
Kathleen-Suzette-Kate-Bell-authors-759206390932120/

https://www.amazon.com/Kathleen-Suzette/e/
B07B7D2S4W/ref=dp_byline_cont_pop_ebooks_1

Made in the USA
Monee, IL
26 February 2025